The author, Brian Townsend, is a 5th grade reading and writing teacher in Chicago, Illinois. He has an undergraduate degree in elementary education and psychology from Marist College in New York, and a Masters of Education from Teachers College, Columbia University in psychological counseling. He lives in Illinois with his wife and kids. *Sessions* is his debut novel.

To Emily; I will never be able to fully thank you, but I will spend the rest of my life trying.

Brian Townsend

SESSIONS

AUSTIN MACAULEY PUBLISHERS™

LONDON • CAMBRIDGE • NEW YORK • SHARJAH

Ordering Information
Quantity sales: Special discounts are available on quantity purchases by corporations, associations, and others. For details, contact the publisher at the address below.

Publisher's Cataloging-in-Publication data
Townsend, Brian
Sessions

ISBN 9781643786988 (Paperback)
ISBN 9781643787206 (Hardback)
ISBN 9781643787534 (ePub e-book)

Library of Congress Control Number: 2020919784

www.austinmacauley.com/us

First Published (2020)
Austin Macauley Publishers LLC
40 Wall Street, 28th Floor
New York, NY 10005
USA

mail-usa@austinmacauley.com
+1 (646) 5125767

First, this book would not have been possible without the unwavering support and love from my wife. Her endless encouragement, multiple proofreads, and frequent reality checks kept me grounded and motivated. Second, I would like to thank all of my friends and family for helping to promote this book.

Chapter 1
October 31st, 2010

Three carved pumpkins line the steps up to the brownstone, as fake cobwebs drape over the side of the stoop. A group of teenagers rush past, loudly laughing while spraying silly string all over each other. I stand here, in my overpriced Wonder Woman costume, on this Brooklyn sidewalk, debating whether I even want to walk up the stairs. Two of the pumpkins are wildly, inappropriately carved, easily the first sign I should have stayed home this Halloween. The third, an intricately carved Hogwarts emblem, just makes me ·feel bad for the poor nerd who made it.

Two slutty nurses walk out the front door, already stumbling over themselves, and with them comes the sound of cheesy Halloween music and muffled conversation from the first-floor apartment.

"I could be binge-watching Parks and Rec right now," I remind Dylan as she sprints up the stairs in excitement and rings the doorbell.

"And you'd be more likely to die a poor old spinster with six cats, so you'll thank me one day," she replies back with that proud smile on her face, as she fixes the slutty indigenous person costume she's ignorantly decided to wear. I hesitate, at the bottom of the stoop, looking around at the crowds of people walking up and down the block. Dylan, frustrated that she's missing out on precious party time, runs back down the steps, places two hands firmly on my back and pushes me up the stairs.

"Oh my god! I'm going. I'm going," I reassure her, moving on my own accord up the stairs. Reaching the front door, sighing heavily, I turn to look at her. "Who are you supposed to be, anyway?"

"Sacajawea," she tells me, as she rings the doorbell. "I thought you'd want me to dress as a strong, independent woman, just like you." She smiles at me. "Look, I get it, you'd rather be living a quiet, boring life, but 23 is a little too young to act like a spinster. Just try to focus on having a good time."

"When have you ever understood my hatred for raging parties?" I accuse her.

"True but that doesn't mean I can't sympathize with your feelings," she admits.

"Empathize," I correct her.

"Exactly," she responds back, clearly not understanding the correction.

"No. You said you could sympathize with my feelings when you should have said empathize. Sympathize is basically feeling sorry for me, but empathize is like being in my shoes and understanding my—"

"Hey, Kevin!" Dylan screeches, like a high school cheerleader as the door opens mid-sentence. Apparently unphased by her misuse of the English language, Dylan jumps into Kevin's arms. Kevin, apparently Dylan's new best friend that she cannot let go of, is dressed in only a Speedo, with goggles and a swim cap resting atop his head.

"Dylan! Wait, wait, don't tell me," Kevin pauses, as I try not to make an NPR joke and completely ruin the whole night. He holds her by the waist and essentially gives Dylan the look down. To be fair, he tried to make it look like he was guessing her costume, but her costume starts at her chest and ends at the top of her thigh, therefore the extended check out didn't need to last that long.

"You must be Pocahontas, right?" Kevin guesses, hesitating at the pronunciation of her name. I can't hold in my laughter and have to turn away from the conversation, pretending I'm coughing.

"Wow, you are good!" Dylan exclaims as she gives him a hug, and winks at me with a beaming smile across her face. "Okay, now my turn," Dylan continues as she releases the hug, but for some reason keeps her hands on his chest and she checks out his costume. "You're that Olympian, the one whose won all the medals. Oh, his name is on the tip of my tongue."

"Michael Phelps," I inform her, knowing that she has a poster of the man hanging on the back of her door. It wasn't the right answer apparently, as she turns to glare at me.

"Ah, common misconception," Kevin replies with a smile, clearly very happy he used the word misconception correctly. "I'm actually Zac Efron, from Baywatch. Can't you see it?" Kevin begins to flex for us, and once again I'm trying to pretend my laughing outburst is a coughing fit.

"Kevin," Dylan awkwardly continues, giving me a disappointed stare as I turn back to meet him. "This is my roommate Alexandra. Alex, this is Kevin."

I stick out my hand as he goes in for the hug. Knowing that he'll cave, I keep my hand out and watch him continue to walk toward me with a goofy smile on his face. He gets about three-quarters of the way there before my stretched-out hand rams right into his rib cage. Realizing I won't budge, he quickly takes a step back, lowers his arms, embarrassingly smiles, and shakes my hand. Just to add to his embarrassment, I make sure my shake is firm, confident, and slightly overpowering.

"Really nice to meet you," he says, just out of politeness since he doesn't think that's true. "Well, guys, c'mon in and help yourself." Like a true, modern man, he walks back inside first, leaving the two of us standing on the porch.

"You aren't dressed as Pocahontas," I remind her as we step into the house and close the door behind us. "What happened to strong, independent woman?"

"Al, look," she begins, with that serious tone in her voice. "Sometimes, you need to build the guy up a little, not tear him down. It's called flirting."

"It's called lying and…" Dylan starts to walk away. "Wait, are you even listening to me?" I ask as she continues to move deeper into the party and waves goodbye as she walks away from my potential TED talk on female empowerment.

The crowd of people stretches out before me, making it look impossible to leave the entryway to the house even if I wanted to. Up on the wall is the American flag, not in a nice frame or folded neatly into a triangle, but just thumb tacked to the wall like it's a poster of some supermodel. It seems unnecessary, a flag representing the country we all live in, like someone might get too drunk and need a reminder, but thinking about Mr. Zac Efron, I'm not surprised it's there.

Besides the flag, the room is scarce of anything resembling grown up furniture. Most people are standing, not by choice though since there are only about six camping chairs spread throughout the living room. They aren't arranged together, like one would think, but they're each placed separately around the room, leaving clusters of people where only one person can sit and the rest need to stand.

There is a large Samsung TV though, since a $1300 television is obviously much more important to these losers than a proper couch. Before I even look at the television, I know what's going to be on it. It's a Friday night at the end of October, and baseball is the only sport interesting enough to have on. There is, of course, a group of four to five man-boys, standing around very enthusiastically cheering every time something good happens for their team. Hanging tightly onto those men are a group of women who are classically being ignored for sports.

"I just love how cute their uniforms look," one blurts out in between a lull in the conversation.

Poor girls.

"Babe," the guy with his arm draped around her replies as chills go up my spine at his use of the word. "The man just threw a massive curve ball. Pay attention."

"Slider," I interject.

In unison, the three guys and the girls hanging onto them all turn to look at me. "Nice try, sweetheart," the one dressed as a shirtless waiter replies. "But that pitch right there, it's called a curveball. That means it curves." His friends laugh, like the idea of him correcting someone is a hilarious joke.

"Actually, no," I reply back smugly. "A curveball is thrown much slower and is released much higher in a pitcher's rotation. For any batter, it's easy to pick out a curveball, but hitting it is more difficult. A slider looks exactly like a fastball, in speed and release point, but breaks as it reaches the plate." The six just stand there with their mouths open, staring at me. "C'mon man, read a book before you pretend to know something." I turn to walk away before I decide to turn back and get one more jab in. "Also, don't even let me hear the word sweetheart come out of your mouth again."

I grab the beer cup from his hand and dump the remaining alcohol into a poorly dying houseplant before tossing his cup back to him. I start to head deeper into the crowd, elbows out, ready to force people out of my way. The lack of clothing on Halloween always shocks me. It's the middle of fall and people are out in fewer clothes than they wear during the summer. Not to mention the lack of clothing, crowded space, and the heat pumping through the vents leads to massive amounts of sweat making the smell of body odor get stronger with each step I take through the crowd.

"Hey! Wonder Woman!" a random guy screams at me as we pass each other, tunneling through the crowd in opposite directions. "You are Wonder Woman, right?"

"No, I'm just carrying around the Lasso of Truth because I'm Batman. Of course I'm Wonder Woman," I reply back, dumbfounded by this idiot's question.

"Oh, OK, cool," he says, "I was just confused because you have long sleeves on. I thought Wonder Woman's outfit was, I don't know, more sexy."

"It's the middle of fall and 40 degrees outside. Why would I..." I stop talking as he walks away, apparently uninterested in my explanation.

Completely unfazed by my lack of sexiness, I continue heading deeper into the party past another group of slutty cats giving me the side eye. At this point, I'm in need of a beer, or something to make this all less awkward. The dining room is a little easier to move around in seeing as everyone is crowding around the table in the corner of the room. A loud cheer erupts from the crowd and a bunch of idiotic fraternity brothers do this odd sort of dance accompanied by some howling. Everyone loves the excitement, since winning beer pong is a clear indicator of one's success in life.

I push past a rambunctious group of sailors and into the surprisingly fancy kitchen that is clearly the highlight of the apartment. Fully stocked with a vast variety of alcohol, the kitchen looks like the place one could do some serious cooking. Seasoning racks completely filled, stainless steel pots and pans, elegant cutting knives—it's like Gordon Ramsey himself lived here. Of course, the elegance is ruined as I move toward the kegs and my feet stick to the floor with each step.

I grab a red cup from the counter and wait behind the chanting men. They continue to count, "56, 57, 58, 59, 60," as two people dressed as Mario and Luigi complete their keg stand with triumphant fists in the air.

"All right, who's next?" a larger gentleman dressed as the Hulk screams. I instantly want to vomit; he stands there, painted green, with massive amounts of unruly chest hair.

I push my way to the front. "Could I just fill my cup up?" I ask.

"Alright, we have one, we still need one more," he states as he scans the crowd.

"Oh no, I think you misunderstood me, I just want to fill up my cup," I inform him, holding the cup up, just in case he's a moron and can't understand what I'm saying.

"Jessica, how about you?" the large man continues. "You want to challenge Wonder Woman?"

Jessica steps to the front of the crowd, dressed as a slutty teacher.

"Look, I literally just want to fill my cup," I remind Mr. Hulk, as two men come up behind me and begin to lift me by my legs. "No, stop. I have no interest in doing this. Put me down."

They continue to lift me as I insist, they stop. They begin to tilt me forwards, holding me toward the keg.

"Stop. Put me down!" I insist, slapping at their hands as they ignore my demands.

"Gentlemen!"

The room stops at the sound of the strong, demanding voice.

"Put her down!"

At this point, I'm completely upside down and can't make out who's speaking. The two men holding me gently lower me to the ground and back away. I stand up, furious at their ignorance. I grab one of the men by the shirt collar and pull him toward my face.

"Listen, you shit; when a woman says no, you listen. You hear me?"

He's shocked, dumbfounded, a deer in the headlights as he simply shakes his head. I let go of his collar and turn to the person standing next to him, the strong voice in the crowd that demanded I was put down. Unlike every other person at this party, all dressed in as minimal clothing as possible, he stands there, completely clothed, dressed in a long Hufflepuff robe, with a wand sticking out of his pocket.

"I'm sorry about that," he sincerely apologizes. "I think they've had a little too much to drink."

"Making an excuse for them doesn't fix the problem," I remind him harshly. "I appreciate you doing the right thing, but I can handle myself."

"Again, I'm sorry. You're right; making an excuse is just enabling the action. I didn't mean to insult you," he again sincerely apologizes. The way he looks at me, it makes me believe him. I instantly want to hate his guts, but for some reason, his soft blues eyes, and the fact that he used *enabling the action* in a sentence, send the message that he's one of the good guys. His soft, kind eyes are stark contrasts to his dominant body posture. He stands tall, proud, but not arrogant, and has a presence that demands attention. I've read all the Harry Potter books, twice, and none of the characters I've pictured have filled out a robe as well as he is right now. I feel this knot form in the pit of my stomach when looking at him, something no man has ever made me feel before.

"I'm sorry," I admit, realizing I was a bit too harsh on him after his attempt to help. "Thank you for the help. I'm Alex."

He sticks out his hand to shake mine, "Mason. Nice to meet you."

His handshake is firm, and he doesn't seem surprised or intimidated by the firmness in my shake as well. In fact, it almost seems to please him, as a happy smile stretches across his face.

"Probably for the best, anyway," the slutty teacher says out loud. "I would have crushed her anyway."

Mason's eyes widen, and a gentle smile crosses his face. We stare at each other for a few seconds, out of disbelief that an "adult" would trash talk over a keg stand.

"Can you hold this please?" I ask him, as I hand him the red cup in my hand.

Taking a ponytail holder out of my pocket, I begin to tie up my hair, continuing to stare into Mason's eyes. He stares back, not impressed, but genuinely happy that I didn't allow a slutty teacher to believe she was better than Wonder Woman.

"Gentlemen," I say, childishly, to the two men who picked me up earlier, "this time, I give you my permission to pick me up. When I give you a thumbs up, that means you put me down. Do you both understand?"

Both of them nod their heads.

"That was a question, boys," I remind them. "Only a verbal yes or no will work. Do you understand?"

"Yes," they both respond back.

The two pick me up from my legs and tilt me toward the keg as I watch them do the same to Jessica out of the corner of my eye. I grab the hose as the group around us begins to count down.

"Three, two, one, go!"

I casually begin drinking as the group continues to count. Blocking out the noise, I try and focus on Mr. Hufflepuff standing against the wall. He isn't chanting, cheering, or counting—he's simply standing there, watching me, with this smile across his face. I watch as two girls walk up to him; one puts her arms around his waist and leans against this shoulder. He turns to look at her and says something to her quickly, but the crowd is too loud for me to hear. Then he turns right back to me, as she lets go of his waist and walks away with her friend. Watching him standing there, I feel this sudden burst of desire— one that I haven't felt in a long time—and it makes me want to talk to him more.

I begin to feel the two men lower me to the ground and turn me right side up. Confused, because I didn't give them the thumbs up, I turn to look at them as they point behind me. The slutty teacher is hunched over the trashcan, throwing up. Everyone, including her friends, stand around and watch like it's some reality show they're invested in. I quickly move toward her, grab the hair from around her ears, and gently rub her back. Not to my surprise, Mason is quickly next to me with a bottle of water.

"All anyone wants to do is stand around and watch these days. Does anybody actually know what helping is?" I ask Mason, completely amazed that people are standing around mesmerized.

"Ladies and gentlemen, I believe they're passing around Fireball in the living room. Better get on that before it's all gone," Mason informs the guests around him.

"Are you really concerned about Fireball right now?" I'm shocked at how stupid I was, believing he was somehow different than every else.

"Relax. Just look," he motions to the kitchen, completely clearing out as the crowd of people head toward the living room.

"Sometimes people just need a little incentive," he says with a smile.

"I underestimated you for a second," I admit to him. "I apologize."

"Isn't the first time, and won't be the last," he explains to me, as he grabs a chair for Jessica to sit on. "That was pretty badass, what you just did."

"The keg stand? Please, that was nothing. We all graduated college. It isn't like it was my first rodeo," I laugh.

"It would have been mine," he confesses, as he hands Jessica the bottle of water and a wet paper towel for her face.

"Wait, you've never done a keg stand?" I ask, amazed by this startling revelation. "You're lying. I'm sure you've done plenty with your frat brothers or whatever."

"Ah," he laughs as he holds up two fingers. "That would be another incorrect judgment on your part, but hey, we're already like five minutes into meeting, so by the time we finish speaking, you'll really only have about 20 mistakes."

"So no keg stands? No frats? Really?" I ask one more time, just to confirm.

"Never in my life."

As he finishes speaking, the man dressed as Zac Efron comes walking toward us.

"Mason," he starts, "I cannot possibly keep dominating this table all night. Please come take my place."

Mason smiles, looks at me, and then turns back to Kevin. "We're a little busy right now," he points down to Jessica, "but put our name down and we'll be out there soon."

Kevin goes to run back to the pong table, but I quickly call him back.

"Kevin, wait!"

He turns around, looks at me like he knows me, but clearly can't remember my name.

"Wonder Woman!" he decides to go with, since he clearly can't mess that up. "What's up? Dylan's over by the pong table if you're looking for her?"

"I'm not. I'm actually wondering if you can help my friend out?" I motion toward Mason, who's staring at me confused.

Kevin laughs, "Ahh, your friend. You mean my *best* friend?" he quickly corrects me.

"Yeah, sure," I brush off his comment and get to the point. "He's apparently never done a keg stand in his life; think you can help me lift him up?"

A giant smile lights up across Kevin's face.

"It would be my greatest joy in life," he responds.

"This isn't happening, we're here for Jessica," Mason tries to remind me as he points down to her.

"Jess, you good?" I ask her. She nods her head and gives a thumbs up as she takes a sip of water. "Perfect. I'll get the left leg, Kevin, you get the right."

Mason squirms at first, but eventually gives in as we lower him toward the keg. He places the nozzle into his mouth as Kevin and I begin to count. I'm quickly aware that watching him makes me happy. Never in my life did I ever think watching someone do a keg stand, in the middle of a Halloween party, standing next to an idiot dressed as Zac Efron, would make me happy.

I'm suddenly glad I didn't stay home and watch Netflix.

After about 30 seconds, he gives us the thumbs up and we lower him gently to the ground. Kevin, anxious about missing his pong shot, runs back toward the table, leaving Mason and I in the kitchen alone. Well, alone with Jessica.

"Thoughts?" I ask him as he wipes the remaining beer from his face.

"Glad to check it off the list," he replies back with a smile.

"Hey, thanks for helping earlier, with Jessica. Most guys I know wouldn't do that," I tell him.

"Maybe you just haven't met the right men," he responds back casually.

Brushing off the sly remark, I start my interrogation of the seemingly perfect man in front of me.

"How exactly did you and Kevin meet?" I ask him.

"Well," he pauses, like he's afraid to admit the truth. "We live together," he responds back, looking slightly embarrassed.

"Wait, wait, wait. You live *here*?" I ask him, completely shocked that such an upstanding person would live in a shit hole like this apartment, but also now aware who made the nerdy Hogwarts pumpkin out front.

"Hold up. I am one of three people who live here. I do not make all of the decisions," he reassures me gently.

"Like the American flag?" I ask judgmentally.

"Like the American flag," he confirms. "I mean we live in America; do we really need to remind people of that every time they walk in the door?"

I smile, amused that his response didn't make me want to walk away from our conversation.

"And the Halloween costume?" I ask, grabbing the wand out of his pocket and waving it through the air.

"You mean my Hufflepuff robe?" he asks, as he strikes a pose. "I'm a wizard. Did you not get that?"

"I didn't grow up under a rock. I've read Harry Potter. I guess, it's just an interesting costume choice given the audience," as I say this, I look around the house at the other men dressed in costume.

"You would like to know why I didn't dress as Zac Efron, or the Hulk," he responds back. "I get it. Why didn't I go with the standard, sexy man costume that all of my fellow men decided to pick? It's a logical question."

"…and the answer is?" I push him, not letting him get away without answering it.

"First off, originality," he begins to explain. "Every guy in this place is trying to show off some part of their body for the sake of attracting a girl…"

"…which you don't need to do," I finish his sentence for him, but also state it for myself. He really doesn't need to show off his body off to attract others. His eyes alone do that.

"Exactly. Secondly, I'm a Harry Potter fanatic and that is the end of this conversation," he finishes with a smile.

"That's nothing to be embarrassed about, I'm sure most people in here loved the movies," I reassure him.

"Ah, there is number three," he responds with a smile, holding up three fingers on his hand. "You assumed I didn't read the books, didn't you?"

"I'm sorry," I respond guiltily. "Not many people read nowadays. Most people just wait for the movies to come out."

"Can I show you my room for a second?" he asks me, seemingly out of nowhere. Here we are, talking about Harry Potter, and suddenly I'm being taken to the bedroom.

Typical.

"Ha!" I laugh while shaking my head in disbelief. "Wow, you really had me convinced for a second. I'll admit you're pretty good, but you lost patience and moved *way* too far ahead."

Mason pauses and bites his lower lip as he holds back a smile.

"I think we're now up to number four," he states as he throws four fingers up again.

"I'm sorry," I reply back laughing. "*That* was a misjudgment? You're telling me that wasn't an attempt to get me alone in your bedroom?"

At that moment, Kevin stumbles over, words slurred.

"Yo, Harry Potter," he mumbles as he stares as Mason's costume, "you and Wonder Woman are up next." He goes to stumble away and then decides he isn't done speaking. "You know he's a total nerd, right?" He's speaking to me now, but his words are so slurred, it's hard to keep up. "Kid's got this monstrous bookshelf in his room filled with books. Nothing else! Just books! Loser!"

This time, Kevin is clearly finished as he stumbles away and back to the beer pong table. I look up at Mason, embarrassed once again. I hold my four fingers up and shrug my shoulders.

"Number four," I confess.

Mason smiles and laughs. "Go hold down our spot on the table. I'll be back in a second." As he speaks, he grabs my hand and gives it a quick, loving squeeze. It's the first time all night we've touched and I hate to admit it, but I hope it isn't the last. There's just something about him. I'm almost afraid of the way he's made me feel like if I continue down this path, there's no coming back. I can't help but smile and stare as he walks away, and out the back door.

"Harry Potter!" Kevin screams, snapping me back to reality. I walk over to the beer pong table, which looks like a pool of alcohol.

"Where's your partner, Wonder Woman?" he asks, leaning against his partner who is clearly the more composed of the two.

"He went out back. He'll be back in a second," I reassure him.

"Ah, boo. Is he smoking without me?" Kevin whines like a baby. "He'll be out there forever. Someone take his place!"

A guy dressed as a doctor, but shirtless under his white coat, steps up to the table. He turns to look at me, gives me a creepy head nod, followed by a smug smile.

"No, no, no…I'm out," I throw my hands in the air and walk away from the table. I start to look for Dylan, but can't seem to find her anywhere in the crowd. Every few seconds, I find myself staring at the back door trying to decide what choice to make. Every ounce of my body is urging me to go out that back door after him, except for my brain. My brain is telling me what it's been telling me all my life.

It isn't worth the risk.

At that moment, Jessica walks up to me and stares at the backdoor with me.

"You're deciding whether to go after him, aren't you?" she asks like she knows the answer I'm going to give.

I nod, my eyes never leaving the back door.

"Why don't you smoke?" she asks a follow-up question, completely out of context.

"What? Is that a serious question? Lung cancer, emphysema, high blood pressure, heart attacks! It's terrible, for you and the environment."

"Do you believe most people in this room know that?" she asks again, as I wait for her to make her point.

"Yes. It's clearly stated everywhere you look how terrible they are for you!" I'm getting heated. I never thought I'd have to explain the health risks related to smoking.

"If people know the risks, why do they still smoke?" she asks.

"I don't know! Stress…addiction. I'm sure there are reasons," I explain to her.

"What's his reason?" she asks, motioning toward the back door.

19

I pause, suddenly realizing her point. An hour ago, I didn't even want to walk into this party, and now, here I am, casting judgments on a seemingly nice person I don't even know. It has become a habit of mine, walking away when things aren't perfect; but looking around at all the people laughing and having a good time, I realize it hasn't gotten me very far in life. It's just made me lonelier.

Smiling at Jessica, I move toward the back door and step outside into the October air. Standing in the distance, shaking his legs to stay warm, is Mason all alone, cigarette in his hand, staring off into the night sky.

"Why do you do it?" I flat out ask him, as I march up to his side. I'm hoping my evident anger will make him tell me the truth. "Why do you smoke?"

He pauses, holds the cigarette at his side, and takes a deep breath.

"Don't lie to me!" I demand. "I deserve to know the truth."

"It's a habit," he declares. Judging by the look on his face, someone's asked him that question before and it must have worked.

"Not good enough," I push back, making sure he knows that answer won't work on me. "What created the habit?"

He stares at me; I'm guessing to figure out whether or not I'm serious. I can see the pain in his face. He's no longer the confident, strong man that he was inside. His eyes are still kind, but I can see there's more to that kindness than what meets the eyes.

"I'm leaving," I tell him and I turn to walk away.

"Wait!" he begs, grabbing my hand.

I shake my hand lose and turn to look at him.

"Give me a reason I should stay," I tell him, making it clear that I get the truth or it will be the last he sees of me.

He looks away, so I turn and walk toward the door.

"I started smoking when I was 15," he begins. I stop dead in my tracks as he continues. "It was something I used to calm myself down. My dad walked out on us and my mom struggled. I took over a lot of responsibility and tried to keep everyone's lives together. I tried, I really did, to keep my own emotions, my own fears out of our home. They weren't going to help anyone. Over time, I needed an outlet, I needed a way to relieve all the tension I had hidden from my family, so I started smoking."

He pauses, takes a deep breath, and closes his eyes.

"It isn't something I do every day. In college, I'd go months without it," he continues, "but sometimes I need an escape, and it's why I've struggled to quit so many times."

Unbelievable.

This whole time, I assume that one act should define my opinion of a person. Every single asshole I've dated, I've met, and I was about to let one act stop me from something that could be amazing.

I hold up five fingers, as Mason stares at me, confused.

"I guess that's misjudgment number five," I say to him as a smile creeps across his face.

"I'd really like to see you again," he tells me, staring at me with those beautiful eyes.

"I might like to see you again, too," I tell him.

"Might?" he asks.

"I will see you again under one condition," I explain to him. "From this moment on, no more cigarettes. I am your cigarette. When you need an escape, a release of your emotions, you come to me. You talk to me, and we will work thought it. Deal?"

I stick my hand out, ready to shake. If this is going to work, this is the only option we have.

A smile creeps across his face; he drops the cigarette to the ground, crushes it with his feet, and shakes my hand.

"Deal," he replies back.

The two of us begin to walk back toward the house.

"Oh," I stop in my tracks and turn around to look at him, "there's one more thing."

He looks, curious about my next request.

"You need to go back and throw that cigarette away. I can't go on a date with someone who litters."

He smiles and turns to walk back toward the last cigarette I will ever see him smoke.

Chapter 2
Session 1

Leaning against the door of the old, beat-up Jeep, I take one last drag of my cigarette, swearing it will be the last drag I ever take. The trees sway back and forth as a gentle breeze blows, urging me to move forward, but I shudder at the thought of having to move any farther. Throwing my cigarette to the ground, even as my gut urges me to get back into the car, I stare out at the path in front of me. The path diverges off the sealed driveway, away from the elegant home resting on the property. The end of the path is not visible from the road, but the directions in my hand reassure me that it is the path I am meant to take. Even if I wanted to doubt the directions, the sign standing tall at the corner of the driveway and path makes it even clearer. It is an arrow, pointing in the direction of the path with the words: Dr. Kimberly McKnight.

Following the gravel path, the shrubs around me get taller and wider the farther I walk. Almost as if a person walking back here would want to disappear from sight, like I desperately want to do right now. The path continues, long and winding, making unnecessary twists and turns, until it abruptly stops at the stoop of the small carriage house. The house, appearing out of nowhere, signals the end of the labyrinth, although looking at the house makes me wish the path continued forever.

Dark green vines snake their way up from the soil, covering the facade of the home. They stretch and spread around the windows and up over the roof of the house. Any white paint that is visible on the front of the house is chipped and decaying, aging it immensely. The vines have grown in a way that makes it look like they are a darkness attempting to drag the house down into the earth.

Then there is the door.

A crisp, freshly painted, red door sits at the top of the stoop, directly in the center of the home. The sight of it feels like a warning, an omen of things to come, or of things that have passed, but I can't figure out which one yet. I desperately want to turn around, walk back through the labyrinth, get into the car, and speed off down the street, far away from here. I know, however, that doing so will only lead me here again.

I also want another cigarette, badly.

Deep breaths, deep breaths. I'll go in, come out, and be finished with this nonsense. I'll do whatever I need to do to never have to come back here again, to continue to live my life.

I pull the silver doorknocker back and let it drop, barely tapping the red door. I'm not afraid to knock loudly, but any excuse to walk away is satisfying enough for me. It isn't my fault if my knock cannot be heard.

I hear footsteps inside shuffle toward the door and hear the lock begin to turn.

Shit.

The door slowly opens and the face of a woman is staring back at me. Her face radiates this energy, almost as if you were looking at a human version of the sun. She isn't smiling or happy, but you can tell the joy she feels to see me standing on her front porch. Her face is rounded, narrowing ever so slightly down to her chin, and her dark-skin makes the colors of her outfit shine brighter. It makes it difficult to focus on anything in the background. Her hair is braided, neatly pulled off to the side with a matching scrunchie, and she has a presence about her. The way she stands is strong, confident, and nothing like you would expect from someone who works in a carriage house like this. Her smile is not only bright but feels safe, like somebody who would still love you while holding onto your deepest, darkest secrets.

"Mason, welcome. Please, come in," she says to me, clearly knowing I would be there. She says it in this warm, quiet voice. Sort of like she's whispering, but she isn't because I can hear her loud as day. It isn't forceful, it isn't commanding, it's just soft.

Welcome.

Please, like this is some goddamn five-star resort in the middle of the Swiss Alps. Don't welcome me here.

Seeing as I can't stand on the stoop forever, I step into the room. As I enter, I quickly realize the sight that spreads out in front of me is nothing like the outside of the house that I just left behind. The room is vast, seeming to expand indefinitely. Unlike the outside of the home, it is fresh, new, and bright. The colors of the wall, the rug, and the furniture make it feel like new. Bookshelves make up the entire back wall, with a ladder that slides from one side to the other. The rows of bookshelves are filled, side-to-side and floor to ceiling, with books. It has been a dream of mine to own a bookshelf like the one before me. I stare, mesmerized by its elegance, as instantly I'm hit with this familiar smell.

"Hope you like it. It's a calming scent for me," she replies, clearly noticing my deep breath in.

"Birch wood," I reply back.

"Yes. It is," she responds. "Most people can't pinpoint what it is."

"My grandfather was a contractor, it's the way his house smelt each weekend when we'd visit. You're a reader?" I ask her, pointing to the books as I hang my light jacket on the coat rack next to me.

"Always have been," she replies back. "I'm not afraid to admit it's mostly fiction, but there's truly nothing like getting lost in a good book."

"Fiction is the only genre of book that exists to me," I reassure her. "Everyone says when you grow up, you're supposed to make this transition to non-fiction, you know, so you can become more worldly or something. I ignore them and stick with what I love."

"I read enough non-fiction in school, no need to continue now," she says with a smile.

Besides the birch wood aroma and the giant stacks of books, the room is filled with tiny, wooden owls. There are easily dozens of them, scattered around on flat surfaces throughout the room. Six rest on top of the fireplace, one on the side table next to the large leather couch, three on the desk in the back of the room, and many more scattered around flat surfaces of the house. All these owls and each one is somehow different from the next. There are some that are sitting, their wings tucked nicely next to them, their eyes observing the world around them. Others are in the midst of flight, their wings spread as wide as possible or about to take off, with their wings beginning to open. Each one a different position, each one a different color, and each one handcrafted with a different style of wood.

"They were my husband's," she states, clearly able to read my facial expression. I need to do a better job of hiding my thoughts.

"The attention to detail is phenomenal," I confess. "Is he a contractor?"

"He was a lawyer for many, many years," she states with the slightest hint of hesitation at the word *was*. "This was just a little side hobby. A way to relieve some stress."

"Why owls?" I ask. Then realizing I may be getting too personal, I add, "If you don't mind me asking."

"What is the first thing you think about when you think of owls?" she asks me. I notice how she doesn't answer the question but simply throws it back into my court. Interested in knowing the answer, I decide to play her little game.

"I always remember hearing how wise they are. I feel like every time I see an owl featured in stories, it's always the wisest one."

"Believe it or not," she responds, with a smile on her face, like that was the answer she was hoping for, "owls are very poor problem solvers. When given cognitive studies, they fail more frequently than many other types of birds."

I notice how she easily uses the word cognitive like it's a word she's used often. I begin to wonder if it was almost used as a way to assert an intellectual dominance, make me trust her a little more because she must be smart. Clearly, she's read more non-fiction books than she's lead on. Nice try, lady.

"They aren't wise?" I ask, confused as to why her husband would proudly brag about loving an unwise creature.

"Aren't they?" she responds with another question in response to a question. She pauses for a minute, staring at one particular owl sitting on the table next to her chair, and then she continues, "What makes someone wise?"

I can instantly tell she's one of those abstract thinkers. One of those people who believe no situation is right or wrong, but a woman who consistently lives in the gray area. I get the sense she's the type of person who won't listen to a friend vent without asking her to think about the other person's perspective.

I hate people like that.

I do not believe in a gray area.

"Knowing all the answers," I respond back matter-of-factly like there couldn't possibly be any other correct response.

"True. Some may say being wise means you can pass the test or solve the problem put in front of you. There are others, however, who believe that simply convincing people you are wise is what truly makes you wise."

There's the gray area.

"So as long as people think you're smart, that makes you smart?" I ask, confused by the statement.

She smiles, pauses, and takes a breath as she configures the perfect response in her head. "As a lawyer, my husband was big on reputation. If the jury believed you, you won your case. The jury isn't going to believe someone they don't see as wise and trustworthy. To him, the owl was a constant reminder that people's perceptions of you are significantly more important than the truth."

"What do you believe?" I ask, completely amazed by her husband's ability to draw such a deep conclusion about an owl and attempting to shift the conversation to her, not me.

"I believe you can only hide the truth for so long," she answers, then hesitates, almost like a memory flashes through her brain. Then she continues, "I make a living on the understanding that what people present on the outside isn't always the truth represented on the inside. To me, the owl is my constant reminder that there is always more than a reputation."

She finishes her words and instantly points to the large, leather couch. Sensing the conversation slipping away, she's attempting to take back control. "Please, have a seat and make yourself comfortable."

I sit down on the large couch quickly, much quicker than I anticipated, almost like our conversation made me forget that I wasn't sitting down across from a friend. It's a comfortable couch, almost too comfortable, like the kind of couch you never want to get up from. I'm no idiot; I know this is how people like her play this game. The welcoming smell, the lighthearted conversation about my family, her husband, the owls, the comfortable couch, and suddenly before you know it, you're spilling your deepest darkest secrets to a stranger you met five minutes ago.

Nice try.

Once I'm seated, she sits down across from me in a smaller, upholstered chair. Next to the chair is a side table, with another finely made owl resting on top. Her favorite owl, judging by its proximity to her, is amid takeoff. Its wings are beginning to open as it starts to push itself off the branch. Oddly enough, it is one of two owls not facing directly forward. This is the first one, turned to face McKnight directly, but the second is sitting right next to me.

"So sorry to waste your time like this," I state as she gets herself settled in her chair, picks up a notebook and pencil, and opens it to a blank page. She pauses as I finish speaking, her notebook page mid-turn, thinks for a second and then finishes turning the page.

"Why would this be a waste of my time?" she asks curiously, like the answer to this particular question is the most pressing matter of our time.

"Well..." I respond and then pause. Shit. I didn't think about how to respond. "I just don't actually think this is necessary, ya know?"

"I'm curious as to what exactly you see as unnecessary," she says, again with that damn curiosity in her voice. Then she pauses, puts the end of her pencil up to her lips, almost like she's trying to make it obvious she's going to speak again. She pulls the pencil away as she continues, "Do you find my job unnecessary, and think I'm wasting my time? Or do you believe you being here is unnecessary, in which case your time would be wasted?"

She doesn't say it forcefully, she doesn't even sound upset. She just states it.

I uncomfortably laugh.

Focus. Focus. Focus. Get back on the message and stick with it.

"Look, I just think there are other things we both could be doing with our time right now. That's all. I hate to waste my own time and I hate to be the reason other people's time is wasted. I'm sure there are plenty of other people you can...ya know...help fix."

26

Perfect.

It gets so quiet in the room that you can make out the sound of the leaves rustling in the wind outside. It makes it feel like my words are just floating around the room, searching for ears to fall upon. I have never hated silence more in my life. I'm waiting for her to respond, to say something while wondering if I offended her, or if I accidentally spilled some secret without even realizing it.

No. I haven't shared anything; just that this is a complete waste. That's not giving anything away…is it?

Finally, she speaks, "What do you consider a waste?"

"I'm sorry?" I laugh lightly again, this time not out of discomfort but because it's kind of a ridiculous question and a loud egregious laugh wouldn't fit this environment. She just continues to stare at me long after the laugh is finished. "I'm not trying to be rude; I just legitimately do not understand that question."

She smiles, "You said that you don't like to waste your time or other people's time and I'm curious about what exactly you consider a waste. For example, do you consider going to the movies a waste?"

"No, not at all," I respond a little defensively. "I actually love going to the movies."

"…but all you do in the movies is sit there. Couldn't that time be spent doing something else?"

"It's a break from the real world, ya know? Movies are entertaining. They're…fun." The answer sounds stupid, but I never thought I'd have to explain the legitimacy of movies to anyone before.

"What if one friend has a problem and they come to talk to you about it, do you consider that a waste?"

"No," I reply adamantly. "There have been plenty of moments I've helped friends and many moments they've helped me."

"…but couldn't you be doing other things?" she asks quickly, throwing my own words back at me again.

"People need you sometimes. You can't control that. It's not a waste if you're helping out a friend. You can't just keep saying, 'You could be doing other things,' because you can say that about anything. 'Oh, I shouldn't waste time eating because I could be doing something else,' or, 'Oh, I shouldn't waste time reading that book because I could be doing something else.' You can always be doing something else." I realize I'm sitting forward on the couch getting heated with the conversation, so I casually lean back against the couch and smile, hoping to send the message that I'm not frustrated.

Even though I slightly am.

"So what I hear you saying is," she pauses and stares off into space, almost like she's trying to remember my exact words, "that sometimes, even though you could be doing something else, you can take a break for different reasons. Is that true?"

"Yes. That is correct."

She jumps in quickly before I can add anything else. "I also hear you say that helping someone else isn't a waste of time. Is that true?"

"Well—" I pause, but she jumps in again before I can continue.

"...is helping others a waste of time? Yes...or no?" It sounds like a demanding question, but the way she phrases it, the way she says it, and the way she looks when she says it almost makes it seem natural.

"No. It's not a waste of time," I reply back.

"Excellent. Now that we have established that you are not wasting your time because you are taking a break and that I am not wasting my time because I am helping someone, let's move forward."

Shit. I fell right into that trap.

"You mentioned earlier," she begins, like earlier wasn't literally four minutes ago, "that I can fix whoever comes into the office. I'm curious—because you are here in this office—does that mean you need something fixed?" Again, when said out of context, it would be insulting to hear, but for some reason, this woman calls me broken and makes it sound like a compliment.

"I don't need anything fixed. I simply meant that people typically come here seeking help for problems, or issues they may need help with." I know fixed was not the right word to use, so I hope the statement backtracks my poorly chosen word and helps her understand my point.

"...and what problem would it be that you need help with?" she asks. It's like she's completely forgotten that I accidentally used the word "fixed" and simply used it as a segway to this exact conversation.

"There is no problem," I respond confidently, sitting a little taller as I inform her of this news.

"...yet you are here?" she asks. It's like she has no idea why a random man showed up on her doorstep even though she was told I was coming. Somehow, she was ready to open the door, and knew my name, but has no idea why I'm here? I wonder if people actually buy this crap.

"I am."

"If people come to this office seeking assistance for problems, and you are here, in this office, that would mean that you are seeking help for a problem, wouldn't it? If A=B and B=C then A=C, right?"

Clearly, someone studied the transitive property in math. I realize I've dug myself into a hole, so I try to stand my ground as firmly as possible.

"I do not need help with a problem," I definitively state again.

"Then why are you here?" she asks like the answer is completely unknown to her.

"Your guess is as good as mine," I tell her.

"You have no clue why you are here?" she asks, completely shocked at my lack of knowledge.

"As I've said, I do not understand why it is necessary for me to be here. It's that simple," I state, hoping to end the conversation in its track. I look away, thinking that maybe breaking eye contact will indicate to her that I'm checked out. Seeing the owl on the side table next to me, I pick it up as a distraction. It's resting, eyes closed, perched on a branch with its wings tucked neatly at its side. The attention to each tiny detail of the owl is remarkable, truly a piece to be admired.

She watches as I examine each mark and blemish. Silence sits in the air and the conversation still seems to linger above us, ready to drop at any second. If I can't exit the conversation, I need to change it.

"I'm amazed by the attention to detail in this owl. I never knew woodworking could produce such results."

Perfect. Focus on the owls.

"It took many, many years of practice before he finally succeeded," she began, not seeming to care about the shift in conversation. "You'll notice certain owls; the ones finished most recently are much more detailed than the ones when he first began."

"Makes sense. Practice makes perfect," I respond, as I place the owl back down on the side table.

"I agree," she says with a smile. It makes me worried I might have cracked the door open for another conversation. "Are you a contractor like your grandfather?" she asks me confidently.

"Uhh…no," I sputter, not expecting a question like that. She continues to stare at me, waiting for the rest of the sentence to come out of my mouth. I wasn't planning on saying anything, but the way she looks, just waiting there, I feel obliged to continue. "I'm in marketing. I'm the Marketing Director for Lincoln Memorial Hospital. My team and I handle all the PR and publicity for the hospital and its doctors."

"When you say you handle the publicity for the doctors, what does that mean exactly?" She asks it with such curiosity that I almost forget where I am. I remember my mother asking similar questions when I got the job all those years ago. Besides her, no one's ever asked such detailed questions.

"Well…let's say a cardiologist performs some groundbreaking surgery and saves the life of a patient by thinking outside the box, being creative, innovative. I would then take the information, compile it in a way for non-doctors to understand and release it to the press."

"…and what would be the purpose of that? What's the end game?" she asks.

"Foot traffic…" I respond.

"Foot traffic?" she asks. I realize it's a phrase we use in the office, but not a phrase commonly used outside. I decide to elaborate a little more.

"My bad…foot traffic is basically patients. When groundbreaking surgeries happen, they typically bring in patients we wouldn't normally see. People who use other hospitals, who are looking for second opinions, stuff like that. A good surgery can really draw in patients from across the globe. You never know when someone from Switzerland is out of options and looking for another perspective."

"That sounds like some really important work you do for the hospital," she responds with a smile. "I imagine that can be difficult in moments when the publicity isn't positive, no?"

It seems like an odd topic to discuss, but I'd much rather talk about my job than whatever else she thinks up. I'll talk about my job for the next 20 minutes if I need to…god, I hope there are only 20 minutes left. I knew I should have brought my watch. Who the hell doesn't have a visible clock?

"Well…yeah. It's happened plenty of times actually," I respond. I finally see a clock, but it is conveniently facing her with its back to me. She sees me glance at it and simply sits there and smiles. Every glance, every deep breath, it's like she's a machine detecting my every subtle move.

"Like when?" she asks in response to my comment about the bad publicity.

"Well, sometimes surgeries go wrong. A risk is taken that shouldn't have been taken, a mistake is made and a patient dies. When situations like that arise, it's my job to clean up the mess."

"Is that difficult for you?" she asks, this time with a more concerned look on her face.

"No…I deal with facts. It's much easier than a doctor dealing with a life or death situation."

"I guess I'm asking because of everything that's happened recently. I'm wondering if doing your job is more difficult now than it was before." She has that serious look on her face. No more smiles or head nods, just her eyes, locked into mine. Finally, after what's felt like forever with continuous small talk, she's gone for the jugular. Like a master at mind manipulation, she casually brought up topics to make me believe I was safe. Yet here I am, staring at her, staring at me, waiting for my response.

"Nothing about my job is difficult. Not now, not before," I state harshly. This conversation will not continue in the direction it is heading and she is poorly mistaken if she believes it will. An undergraduate degree from Harvard, master's from Princeton, I'm no idiot. I didn't build a life, a career based on sharing personal details with strangers in their homes while they take notes on my every move.

"I apologize if the question seemed forward," she begins in a sincere apologetic tone, "but as you mentioned earlier, practice makes perfect. It is a question that needed to be asked." The second part of the sentence sounds much more assertive, demanding, instructional. Almost like a prediction that the question will get answered whether or not I am willing to answer it.

"The question was not an issue," I reassure her, making sure she can't sense the anger in my tone.

"Humor me for a second, if you will. Take a look at your hands," she states. "Don't move them, just look." Her facial expression has remained the same this entire time. Through the conflict, the tension, the heat that I feel rise up in the room, she's been unfazed. Her posture, body position, facial expressions have been constant. Yet, I look down at my hands and I instantly notice what she hopes I will see. My hands, once flat and resting gently on top of my thighs, are now balled, clenched. I have not stayed constant throughout the tension, the heat. Not only did I react, but I reacted in a way that signals anger, which has already told her too much about me.

"Do you consider yourself an angry person, Mason?" she asks, like she's genuinely interested in my opinion on the topic. She doesn't, however, give me a chance to give that opinion. "Typically when I see clenched fists, like yours, it signals that the conversation brought up some unresolved emotions."

"I am not an angry person. I get angry just as much as other people," I respond back shortly, which doesn't help me prove a lack of anger.

"I know you said you felt like this was a waste of time, but if you had to pick an emotion that represents how you feel about being here, which one would you pick?" she asks.

"Isn't feeling like it's a waste of time an emotion?" I know the answer, but I try to avoid the question anyway.

"No," she responds with a light laugh to try and lighten the mood and ease my discomfort. "Emotions are feelings, like happiness or sadness, frustration or joy. If you had to put a word to your emotions, right now, how would you feel?"

"Confused," I respond back, unaware if confused is truly a feeling, but figuring it might buy me some time until the end of the session.

"Confused, really?" She nods, "That's fascinating."

Now I'm legitimately confused.

"I'm sorry, what makes confused so fascinating?" I ask back aggressively.

"One of the most eye-opening non-fiction books I read in school was about Gandhi and his view of human emotions," she states as she gets up and heads toward the bookshelf. I'm silent as she rummages through the shelves, looking for a book. "I purposefully organized the books by the Dewy Decimal System, so if I ever needed to find something, I'd know exactly where it will be."

Now it just seems like she's bragging.

"Ah!" she exclaims as she pulls a book from the shelf. She brings it back to her seat and holds it out to me. "There's a belief that Gandhi and many in the psychology community share, that confusion isn't actually a human emotion. It isn't something you can feel."

She's telling me all this, yet the book is resting closed on my lap. She didn't even need it, but somehow, I feel she wanted me to know it existed.

"Gandhi believes that when humans are confused, it simply means they are stuck between two different emotions. For example, I feel fear about going on the rollercoaster because I've never been, but I also feel joy about doing something for the first time. That leads me to be confused because I'm stuck between two different emotions."

"That's great, but what does that have to do with me?" I ask, uninterested in her babbling.

"Your confusion means that deep down, subconsciously, you're caught between two different emotions. You don't know which one to feel more, so you develop this sense of confusion," she explains, like a college professor would to her pupils.

"That all sounds great," I respond back, this time not hiding my bitterness, "and maybe it works on all of your less intelligent, attention-seeking patients. It doesn't work on me. I am confused, yes, because I don't understand why I need to waste my time sitting here with you acting like I'm a goddamn mess."

Silence.

"You remind me of a soldier," she states. When she says it, it doesn't sound like a compliment, yet it's a statement that is hard to take offense to. "You sit up, tall, and strong. You purposefully make yourself uncomfortable on what I personally believe is *the* most comfortable couch in the world. Most importantly, you put yourself in a position where you are constantly on your toes. It's typically done to maintain control, to maintain power."

"I don't believe in being the weakest person in the room," I tell her. I decide to be honest and open for the first time. It was a lesson from my father long ago, but she doesn't need to know that.

"When you say weakest, what do you mean? Because physically, I don't think you need to worry about being the weakest in the room often," she replies, again not missing a single detail about me.

"I work hard to maintain a physical presence, yeah, but it's more than just physical. Weaknesses often don't come from a lack of physical strength," I inform her. "They actually more often come from inside. Internal weaknesses are the downfall of the strongest men. The weak succumb to comfortability in unfamiliar situations. They get so comfortable that they lose sight of their opponent, of the goal, and before they realize it, they've been beaten."

"Spoken like a true athlete," she says with a smile—almost like my rant was amusing to her.

"All-American swimmer. High school and college," I inform her. "I know what it feels like to get too comfortable and lose, but I also know what it feels like to stay aware and win."

"Is that what you are trying to do here? Stay aware and win?" she asks me. It's a question I wasn't expecting. I guess that's the epitome of this conversation, questions that I don't expect. Makes it harder to prepare, but doesn't make it impossible.

"I try to make sure I am in control at all times," I tell her. "Not just here in this room, but outside of this room as well."

"I see," she says, as that serious look crosses back onto her face. Up until this point, she had seemed interested, curious in what I was saying, but suddenly she's concerned, serious. I brace for what she might say next. "Is that what you were doing last month when you were arrested? Was that 'being in control?'"

The jugular.

This whole damn time, trying to avoid conversation, to dodge questions, to avoid giving away the tiniest of details, and here we are, at the heart of it all. I played directly into her hands.

Or did I?

Did it matter what I said, or what direction the conversation went in? Did it matter if I got comfortable on this damn comfortable couch or sat like I had a stick up my ass? Did it matter that I tried to anticipate every move she made before she made it?

Or was she that good that we were going to get to this point no matter what?

"I only ask," she continues, my blank stare a clear indicator of my shock, "because in here, to me, it seems safer to get uncomfortable, to lose control, than it would be to lose control…in, let's say…a grocery store?"

It clearly is a rhetorical question, yet I feel the need to respond. I continue to sit there, now aware that my hands have clenched even tighter than before.

Focus. Deep breaths. Control.

Think. Think. Think.

She speaks before I have the chance, almost like kicking someone while they're down. I guess I'm not the only one who knows what it takes to be the strongest person in the room. I've underestimated her and right now, she's winning.

"The owl," she begins, "may be wise because it convinces people it is wise, but when you put it in a cage with a hanging string and make it pull the string to earn food, it will die. It dies because its truth is exposed. It is not wise. It is, in fact, unable to continue to survive when tested."

She stops speaking and the silence hangs in the air. There is no further explanation, no more speaking; there is only the silence that not only lingers but expands the longer we wait. Like a conquering hero, it spreads across the couch, to the window, to the fireplace, and over every single owl in the room. The silence envelops each crevasse of the room and into the depths of my soul. It can only be broken by the words stuck inside my throat. The words I wish I knew how to say, I wish I knew how to formulate, but the words that sit there, like boulders crushing my esophagus.

We stare…well, she stares. Each second the silence remains; she continues to stare. She's reading me, reading my blank expression, reading my glazed over eyes, reading my struggle to speak. The pressure from the words inside my throat, now invading my body like a disease, spread with the intent to kill. I'm struggling to breathe as my chest starts to cave. The longer I sit here in this silence, the closer I feel to death.

Then, she drags me back from the depths of hell.

"That's all the time we have for today, Mason. We've made great progress. Practice makes perfect. I look forward to seeing you next week."

I stand, numb throughout my body. She shakes my hand with a smile on her face like it's been a pleasant meeting of friends and then she opens the door, hands me my jacket, and sends me into the world as the darkness of night begins to take over.

As I step out onto the porch, I turn to look at her.

At that moment, I realize…she won.

And it is at that moment the red door closes.

34

Chapter 3

Dontrell Williams' mind was calm as his body rested, bent over on the starting blocks with his fingers tapping gently, waiting for the gun. A hush fell over the crowd as they anxiously anticipated the start of the championship race. Even staring straight down into the pool, he could feel everyone's eyes directed to his lane. He imagined his father, standing next to the college scouts, arms crossed, brow furrowed, his fear of being embarrassed even greater than his nerves for his son racing below. The only person he knew wasn't ready for this race to start was his mother. Three rows up into the bleachers and a few seats down from the aisle, he knew his mother was staring at the floor just like him. It was like she could feel his nerves, and was suffering the same nauseous feeling he felt in his stomach each time he raced. As excited as everyone around her was, as excited as his father was, Dontrell knew his mother saw this as just another race. Win, or lose, nothing about this raced changed anything.

That's what Dontrell chose to believe.

The gun sounded and like an instinct, Dontrell pushed his body off the starting block, the heated water warming up his hands, then his head, and finally down to his feet as it enveloped his body.

Seven seconds, seven seconds, he kept saying to himself, hoping to will his body to get to the 15-meter mark as he floated his way to the surface. This was his favorite part of every race; the silence. Forget the joy of finishing, the silence that lived under the water was what made him fall in love with swimming so many years ago. The screams from above are simply inaudible, no match for the denseness of the water.

"7.4 seconds!" he hears his father call out the instant his head reaches the surface. "Too slow, too slow!"

Another reason why the silence underwater felt golden.

Baffled by his father's ability to make himself heard over an entire crowd, Dontrell chose to ignore the comment as best as he could.

Gabbing the water as he moved along, Dontrell could see the other competitors each time he turned his head. Henry Zucar, the most talked-about swimmer in the state was in the lane next to him. Widely considered New York's golden swimmer, Zucar had beaten every kid in the state twice, except for Dontrell. The only caveat was they never actually swam against each other. Today was the day Dontrell was trying to prove he was the best swimmer in the building. Zucar, however, was trying to do the same. The question was, who would end up on top? There were at least seven—Dontrell counted—college scouts who eagerly showed up to wait for the answer.

Close to 50 yards in, Dontrell spotted the "T" on the bottom of the pool, so he prepared himself, knowing the turn would either make or break this race. Flipping his body and pushing against the wall with any strength he had left, he coasted underwater preparing to surface—the silence, once again, calming his mind.

The second he got to the surface; he heard his voice again. "Decent turn, decent turn!" his father screamed from the crowd.

'Decent?' Dontrell wondered to himself. *'That was easily the best turn of my career.'*

Ignoring the lack of encouragement coming from his father, he continued to push harder and harder. As he turned his head for air, he quickly spotted his mother sitting on the bleachers. Unlike his father, she was quiet. She sat there with her hands covering her mouth, watching his every move. While his father looked for technical mistakes with each individual stroke, his mother watched the race as a whole. She saw the whole picture, from start to finish. It's not that she didn't catch the small, minute errors—she noticed each time his body tensed up, or when his breath count was off, but she was smart enough to realize nothing can be perfect.

It was her encouragement, not his father's criticism that made him the swimmer he is today. All those summers on the lake, swimming from the shore to the dock while she stood there, the water up to her knees, encouraging them with each stroke. He knew she wished she could be swimming right next to them, but her inability to swim only made her more proud when he would experience any little success. Meanwhile, his father would sit on a lounge chair on the beach, his paper in his lap, yelling out the mistakes he made every few minutes. It wasn't that he knew how to swim, it was simply his belief that he needed to be a hard-ass father for his children to be successful. People thought they were crazy, going on the same vacation year after year, but his parents never stopped to listen to the opinions of others. The lake was a second home for him and his brother. It was where they learned to swim for the very first time, and where they continued to practice getting better and better. Now here she was, following both of her children weekend after weekend, around the country to watch them swim.

The lactic acid started to build up, as Dontrell felt his legs getting heavier and heavier. Less than 25 yards left and he could sense Zucar pulling away. It was even more evident from his father's excessive yelling.

"Faster! Faster!"

With one last surge of energy, Dontrell began to close the gap. Twenty yards left as his legs fluttered at top speed. Fifteen yards left as he surfaced for much-needed oxygen. Ten yards left as his mother, still covering her mouth with her hands, stood up in the crowd. Five yards left as the rings separating the lanes begin to change colors. His legs burning as the lactic acid spread like wildfire. Finally, Dontrell reached out, as far as his arms would allow while still kicking his legs full force. He reached for the wall and felt a wave of relief when his fingertips touch the solid surface.

Done.

All he can hear is his own heartbeat and the sound of himself breathing. There were anxious murmurs coming from the crowd, awaiting the final results. He ignored them for a second and put his face back underwater one last time. He floated there, soaking in the silence before his overworked lungs forced him to take another breath. Taking his swim cap off his head, the roar of the crowd intensified as the final times popped up on the scoreboard. Dontrell focused on his breath, hanging on the lane line for support, his body feeling limp. Without even looking at the scoreboard, he shook Zucar's hand, commended him on a good race, and gave him a tired smile.

Sportsmanship first. That was his mother's first rule. No matter how many times Dontrell and his brother, Kemarion, raced at that lake, no matter how heated the competitions got, she would always force them to look each other in the eye, shake each other's hands, and say "good job." Even when they were mortal enemies, convinced the other cheated their way to victory, their mother would make them sit next to each other around the fire, and forcing them to share a stick to roast marshmellows. At the end of the day, she would tell them, "It is only a race."

First, Dontrell looked to his father, already turned around, facing the opposite direction of the pool probably making some excuse to the college scouts who still hovered around him. Then he saw his mother, hands now behind her head with a giant smile on her face. Last, he looked at the scoreboard, but he already knew what it said.

His time, faster than any high school swimmer had swum before, was over a second faster than his own personal best time. On any given day, the race would have been considered a huge accomplishment. The only problem was today wasn't any given day, and today, it was only good enough for second place by two-tenths of a second.

Everyone in the room stood on their feet, and the excitement was evident in their faces. They screamed and hollered, astonished that two swimmers just put up two of the fastest times ever for high school athletes. Getting out of the pool, Dontrell was crowded with teammates slapping him on the back, congratulating him on a great race. He smiled and thanked them, still struggling to catch his breath and desperately wanting to sit down. Grabbing his towel, Dontrell headed over to the side of the pool. Standing there with arms wide open, and the biggest smile on her face, his mother wrapped him up tight.

"I am so proud of you," she told him, squeezing him even harder. "That was the best race I've ever seen from you." It was a fact that carried weight, seeing that she hadn't missed a single one of his swimming races since he started over 12 years ago. She continued to hold onto him, cherishing the moment.

"Mom," he begged, "mom, please let me go. I can't breathe." Finally, his mother let go, just as his father approached.

"You could've had him!" the first words that come out of his mouth as he shook his hand. "I'm telling you, if you just listened to me last time, you could've had him!"

"There's nothing I could have done, Dad," Dontrell expressed exhaustively, looking around the pool to find somewhere else to go, someone else to talk to.

"Nothing?" his dad questioned. "I told you exactly what to do last week and you didn't listen. I told you the first 15 have to be seven seconds or faster. Get off those blocks. If you just did that, you would've won."

"Can we not do this right now?" Dontrell asked. "I'm tired and really don't want to hear it."

His father took a deep breath and reached his hands into his pockets, one of his many signs of swallowed anger. Dontrell took it as a good sign to leave. "I'm going to go jog around for a cool down. My legs feel pretty beat," he told his parents.

"Great job, honey," his mother reminded him again.

"At least ten full minutes, otherwise those legs will be trash all week," his father called out, as his wife's hand gently slapped the front of his chest. "What? It's the truth."

"Sometimes," she explained to him, "he just needs to be left alone."

"Kemarion would have listened to me," his father explained. "He knew I was only trying to help. He always listened. Heck, he'd even ask for my advice."

"And Dontrell is not the same person," she reminded him. "Just because they're brothers, doesn't mean you can take the same approach."

Dontrell began to head outside, throwing on his sweats and a hoodie, when a man in a Stanford pullover called his name and approached.

"Hiya! John Hanigan," he stated, sticking his hand out to shake. "I'm an assistant coach at Stanford."

Over the coach's shoulder, he could see his father smile and put two thumbs up in the air, a sign of excitement over the fact that someone from his alma mater was recruiting his son.

"Oh," Dontrell replied, "hey. Really nice to meet you."

"Please, the pleasure is all mine," Hanigan stated. "Listen, I don't want to keep you. I know you've got to cool down. Just wanted to let you know we were very impressed with the season you had this year and we'd be very interested in flying you out over the next few months to show you around the school."

Shocked, Dontrell struggled to find the right words. "Wow. That's really kind of you. Thank you for coming out to watch. I'm sorry it didn't go as planned."

Hanigan laughed. "Ah, we've both been swimming long enough to know that you can't win them all. Second place at the Olympics still gets a medal, right? Don't be too hard on yourself."

Dontrell smirked, "That's a good way to look at it."

"Look," Hanigan stated very matter-of-factly, "we're kicking ourselves for missing the boat on your brother. That day he won the NCAA Championship, he really reminded us how wrong we were when we didn't recruit him intensely. We don't want to make the same mistake with you. I'll be reaching out over the next couple of weeks and I look forward to continuing this conversation."

He shook his hand and walked back toward the pool, waiting to watch the other races still to come. Dontrell opened the door and stepped out into the frigid January air. The mounds of snow piled in the school parking lot were just one sign of the rough winter. Dontrell longed for the spring days where shorts and a t-shirt were appropriate running attire.

"Williams!" Jacob Johnson called out, jogging in the distance.

"JJ!" Dontrell replied. "How's it going, man?"

JJ ran over to join Dontrell and the two began to cool down. "Was that the Stanford coach?" he asked Dontrell.

"Assistant, but yeah, it was," Dontrell replied. "He just wanted to tell me good job, that's all."

"Aren't they the best in the country?" JJ asked.

"One of," he replied. "Kemarion told me last year they won the National Championship, but he didn't think they would this year."

"Did Kemarion even get offers from Stanford?" JJ wondered.

"Nah," Dontrell laughed, "I think it was the one school he really wanted it from, but he never got it."

"California in the winter sounds a lot better than New York right now," JJ admitted. "You hear about the storm that's supposed to hit?"

He hadn't. Between the countless hours spent in the pool each morning before school and in the evening's after school, he didn't have much time to keep tabs on the weather. Swim practice was rain or shine, so the weather wasn't a concern of his, plus passing AP Chemistry seemed like it was more deserving of his time at the moment.

"I actually haven't," he confessed to JJ. "I've been stuck studying for Mr. Pedroia's chemistry midterm. That class has been kicking my ass."

"You? Struggling?" JJ asked in amazement. "Aren't you a straight-A student?"

Dontrell laughed, "I won't be if I don't pass this midterm. I don't know what it is, but I just can't wrap my brain around molecular formulas. You'd think it would be like math, but it's so unbelievably complicated."

"You should come over tonight to study," JJ said. "I got a 90 on the quiz we took on it last week, so I've got a good handle on it. We can study a little and then head over to Elizabeth's party if you're interested."

"She's having another party?" Dontrell asked, surprised. "Are her parents ever home?"

"Man, you know how some of these families around here are," JJ explained. "They leave their kids nonstop to go vacationing like it's a second job."

"I don't know, man," Dontrell admitted. "I'd have to work on convincing my dad to let me go out. He usually puts his foot down after meets."

"Look, just try to convince him, and let me know," JJ responded.

Dontrell knew the odds of being allowed out were slim, especially to a party, but he promised JJ he'd let him know. As the two rounded the corner of the building, finishing up their cool down, Dontrell's parents were standing at the door.

"I said ten minutes," his dad called out. "Don't you have a watch? Clearly, it's been 15. Hurry up and change. If we don't get food inside you quickly, those legs will be trash all week."

Ignoring his father's comments, Dontrell said goodbye to JJ and headed back inside with his parents. He grabbed his duffel bag and walked into the locker room to change. All he could think about was the amazing opportunity

Stanford could provide him, but deep down he knew the greatest thing Stanford could offer was distance from his father.

———

Sitting in his beanbag chair, the PlayStation controller in his lap, Dontrell could see the snowflakes begin to fall outside his bedroom window. Lounging back, his feet elevated against the dresser, he closed out his 2K17 game with a massive, game-winning three-pointer from Kyrie Irving. The trophies and medals from years of swimming flooded his room, resting on each and every possible surface. Newspaper clippings covered the walls, some declaring the Williams brothers the protégés of the swimming world, many chronicling Dontrell's latest high school triumphs, and others detailing his painful tribulations. Those painful articles, hung there by his father to continue to remind him about the feeling of losing, were few and far between. Just as he was about to start another game, he heard a firm, hard knock on the door. Dropping the controller to the floor, he swiftly turned the TV off and leaped onto his bed; an AP Chemistry book sat there, already opened to a random page.

"C'mon in!" he announced, knowing it was his father. His mother never knocked. She'd announce halfway down the hallway that she was entering the room, and then she'd fling the door wide open and walk right in. With his father, however, things were always more formal. It wasn't always that way, but somewhere around middle school, Dontrell felt the relationship change. While his conversations with his mother continued to flow, the ones with his father felt forced, like pulling teeth. It got much worse when Kemarion left for college. The two talked constantly, mostly because Kemarion loved talking about swimming and nothing else. When he left, his father directed all that energy toward Dontrell, with much less success.

"I'm coming in," his father announced back awkwardly.

"Yeah, that's fine," Dontrell repeated. "C'mon in."

His father opened the door slowly, poking his head in first, but never fully stepping into the room.

"You should have those legs elevated," he stated, clearly unaware of how to have a conversation with his son about anything other than swimming.

"Yeah. I just had them up for ten minutes," Dontrell replied. "They're good to go."

His father looked down at the PlayStation remote on the floor. "Make sure you're studying for that midterm. We can't afford any B's on that report card if we're going to get into Stanford."

It was always "we" with his father like he was living inside Dontrell's body or at least trying to live vicariously through him. "*I*," Dontrell reminded him, "will be fine. I've got a study session set up tonight with JJ."

"Jacob Johnson?" his father asked. "Isn't that the boy you were jogging with today at the swim meet? Why would you study with him? You know what, you should go study with Jesse Kim, or one of his friends."

"You're joking, right?" Dontrell asked dumbfounded. "Why can't I study with Jacob, but I can study with Jesse Kim?"

His father stood there silently, struggling the find the right words. Dontrell could feel the wheels in his brain turning, flipping through line after line wondering which one was the correct choice. He could also see tightness in his father's face as he took a deep breath in an attempt to control his anger and reached into his pocket.

"All I'm saying," his father stated with a little shaking evident in his voice, "is that Jesse Kim would be a great study partner. His father's a highly successful doctor. JJ's father's a mechanic. Who do you think knows more about science?"

This time, Dontrell took a deep breath to control his own anger. "How about if I promise I won't get a B, you let me just go study with whoever I want?"

"Stanford won't stand for B's," his father stated boldly. His anger continued to swell as his voice got louder with each word he spoke. "I talked a big game to those scouts today, and I don't want to be embarrassed. I know you think the world's going to fall into your lap, but you have to work for things. I didn't become successful by sitting on my ass playing video games."

"Derrick!" his mother yelled from downstairs. "It's almost six! You don't want to be late for your meeting."

His father took a deep breath, took one last look at his son, and walked away. Thankful that his mother sensed the impending argument, Dontrell got back up and stood in the doorway, watching his father walk away, fists clenched, visibly upset with the conversation.

"Dontrell! Dinner!" his mother called upstairs.

Quickly changing from his sweats to jeans and throwing on a button-down shirt, Dontrell grabbed his phone and headed downstairs. As he headed to the kitchen, his phone buzzed.

"What are you up to tonight?" it read.

"Studying with JJ and then possibly Elizabeth's party. See you there?" he responded back.

"You need to be kinder to your father," his mother interrupted as he sat down at the kitchen table. "You know he's trying his best." She placed a plate of chicken and broccoli in front of his seat as he pulled out the chair to sit down.

"Is he though?" Dontrell asked. "If that's trying his best, I'd love to see what average would be." He never hid his feelings about his father from his mother, and he also never understood how she had the patience to deal with him. Always the self-reflective person, she handled the rocky relationship between her husband and son perfectly, continuing to push the other to be kinder.

"I just want you to put yourself in his shoes," she told him, sitting down to eat herself. "He's fighting a battle that we cannot see each and every day."

"Sometimes, I think he'd be better if he drank," Dontrell blurted out, regretting the statement the moment it came out of his mouth.

"You don't mean that," his mother said kindly. She could have blown up, yelled at him, and lectured him about the comment, but she already knew how badly he felt about saying it. "Just continue to support him any way you can."

As she finished speaking, the buzzer on Dontrell's phone went off again. He looked at it quickly, smiled, and then placed it back face down on the table.

"Is that Henry?" his mother asked gently, keeping her eyes focused on her meal, moving the broccoli around with her fork. "What is he up to tonight?"

Dontrell paused, wondering why she was asking, then decided to answer her question. "Yeah. He's heading to a party over on Patterson Street. It's at Elizabeth Caraveli's house. You remember her, from elementary school? The redhead."

His mother laughed, "I don't think she'd like you to refer to her as the redhead."

Dontrell laughed with her, "Yeah, but we both know she refers to me as the black kid to her parents, so I feel less bad about it."

His mother laughed even louder, knowing that it was true. "I overheard you might be studying with JJ? He's in AP Chem with you?"

Dontrell placed some chicken in his mouth. "Yeah. I was going to ask if it was okay for me to go over and study there. We have a midterm coming up next week that I want to make sure I'm ready for. Plus, he really understands molecular equations and you know how badly I've been struggling with them."

"Of course," his mother replied. "Is that the only place you'll be going?" It was like she knew. His mother was always someone who had that mother's intuition. She knew the answer but wanted him to be honest about it.

"Well…" Dontrell began, wondering how to bring up the party. "I was also going to ask if I could go to Elizabeth's party. JJ and I were going to head over after we studied since it's just over the tracks from his house. I know what you're thinking and no, her parents won't be home." Dontrell decided to be honest with her. He had never lied to her in his life and he wasn't going to start now. "Kids will be drinking, but as you know, I will not. I promise you. I will not drink."

His mother touched his hand, looked up at him and smiled. "Yes, you can go. I know you will not drink, nor do I want you to drink, but I do hope that one day you will feel comfortable enough to have one."

Dontrell squeezed his mother's hand before standing up and taking the plates to the sink. By the time he was done washing the dishes and cleaning up from dinner, he kissed his mother goodbye and headed out the door for JJ's.

"Be home before curfew," she yelled out to him. "And Dontrell, say hi to Henry for me…he's such a nice boy."

Dontrell waved back as confirmation, still wondering why his mother continued to bring Henry into the conversation and concerned that, once again, it was due to her intuition. He got into his gray, beat-up sedan and began the short drive to JJ's. The whole ride, he thought about the night his mother was going to have all alone. He hated that feeling, the one he had whenever he'd picture her sitting on the couch all by herself. It pained him to think that this woman built an entire life for her family, raised two respected and kind children, and still managed to keep a recovering alcoholic sober. Each night, however, she'd spend her time alone. Most nights, it was that feeling that forced Dontrell to stay home, but he also knew that he had to be a kid. It wasn't his responsibility…it was his father's. His mother didn't need a son's company, she needed a partner's company and his father failed to provide that for her.

Deep down, he hated the life that his father's illness created for his mother, but she never seemed to care. His mother was the rock of the family, the caregiver, the backbone. Without her, neither him, nor his brother, would be where they are today, but that was especially true for his father. All those years ago, when she first discovered his disease, she'd mark all the bottles in the house and check each night. It was her proof when she first confronted him about it, and the proof when he fell off the wagon twice. Still to this day, any alcohol in the house was marked and measured.

Dontrell pulled up to JJ's house—a small, well kept, one-story ranch just on the other side of Main Street. The houses around JJ's, with overgrown lawns and broken windows, didn't even compare to the appearance of his house. Broken streetlights littered the street, but JJ's house stood out like the beacon of hope in a struggling section of town. Reaching in the back to grab his chemistry book, he felt his phone vibrate in his pocket. He reached for it and pulled it out as a text flashed across the screen.

"I'll be there. Excited to see you tonight," it read.

A smile flashed across Dontrell's face as he placed the phone back into his pocket.

Chapter 4
November 7th, 2010

Butterflies.

Looking at them, nothing about their presence would make me nervous. I see these beautiful, elegant creatures relishing in their life's transformation and feel nothing but hope. A butterfly is a perfect metaphor for evolving, changing, becoming who you were born to be. The way a butterfly changes and grows from this ugly, small, overlooked creature into an attention-demanding beauty will always impress me. I've just never seen them as a sign of nerves.

At least not for me.

For me, the way I'm feeling, it's what others would describe as butterflies in my stomach.

I'd like to respectfully disagree.

Maybe the interpretation has changed over the years, but to me, if I had thousands of butterflies in my stomach, I imagine it would feel exhilarating. I imagine I'd feel this overt sense of joy. Butterflies in your stomach is a phrase that should be used when you feel so happy, so light like your joy could lift you off the ground you're standing on and whisk you away. Too often, the term butterflies in our stomach is used in scary, dangerous situations, like in horror films, when we are unsure if the lead character should walk into the dark, scary dungeon, or when we're about to go take the largest test of our lives. Those don't seem like happy, butterfly in your stomach moments to me; they seem like scary, nerve-racking ones.

Like spiders in your stomach.

Now that sounds like a good description of a scary, nerve-wracking moment.

It also sums up how I'm feeling right about now.

Standing in the living room, trying not to peek out the blinds every few seconds, I pace back and forth. I peek out really quickly, not that I expect to see anything since there are still 20 minutes until my date should arrive. I can't help it, though. I keep telling myself to calm down, to act normal and not like some crazed out 16-year-old girl.

"Now you're sure you're happy with the outfit?" Dylan asks me, as she sits on the couch, a pint of ice cream in her hand and a spoon hanging from her mouth. Her eyes are still locked onto the television as a screaming match ensues on Real Housewives of Beverly Hills. "It just seems like maybe you should put in a little more effort to impress him."

Sometimes, I don't even know how to respond to her. Somewhere along the line, for most women I've met, it's been ingrained in their mind that a date is their opportunity to show a man they're worth it. There's a belief that by dressing up, acting a part, and impressing a man, that can lead to future happiness.

How can that be? How is acting like someone you aren't or proving that you are worthy, leading to a happy life?

"If he's going to like me," I inform her, "he's going to like me for exactly who I am."

"Yeah, but you need to make him want a second date," she informs me, swallowing another heaping of ice cream.

"He needs to make me want a second date," I remind her. "This is a two-way street. He needs to impress me just as much as I need to impress him."

"You think he's going to try to kiss you?" she asks.

"Ha! I hope he does. I'd love nothing more than to shut him down."

At this comment, she pauses the TV and stares at me, "Why would you do that?"

"I can't kiss him on the first date," I tell her. "I need to make him work for it."

"You're telling me, even if he's the most charming man you've ever met, you still won't kiss him?" she asks me, shocked.

I smile, as I peer out the shades one more time, just checking to see if he's early. "The only way this man is leaving with a kiss tonight," I respond, "is if I'm convinced he's the love of my life. He's got to be more than just charming. I'm not looking for a prince. I want a partner."

"High standards," she tells me, picking up her phone and responding to a text. "I'd take a prince any day…especially Harry."

I turn back to the window, astounded that these types of conversations still happen today. It's the age of feminism, of women having it all and doing it all. It's astonishing how slowly ingrained stereotypes take to disappear.

The spiders in my stomach intensify as I hear the doorbell ring. Already pleased with his punctuality, I grab my purse and blow Dylan a kiss as she makes wildly inappropriate sexual gestures on the couch. As I open the door, she calls out, "Have her home by midnight!"

I slam the door shut quickly behind me, ashamed and embarrassed that he heard.

"Wow," he tells me before I even get a chance to look up, "you look amazing."

I find myself smiling. Even in this age of feminism, I still can't help but smile when someone tells me I look nice. Noticing how he used the word amazing and not pretty impresses me. Most women would be unhappy with that word, but I appreciate its broadness. Only a woman can be pretty, anyone can look amazing.

Speaking of amazing.

The Harry Potter nerd from the week before has, like the caterpillar, completed evolved. He has a tall, firm presence, not in a towering, threatening way, but in a confident, protective way. His shoulders are broad, while his waist is narrow, which is strikingly evident in his form-fitting jacket and skinny jeans. He, similar to me, looks comfortable, not flashy. "Well, you don't look like a wizard anymore," I tell him as we walk down the stoop.

"Yeah, you know, sometimes I like to just take the robe off, relax a little," he jokes.

"It's a beautiful night," I tell him, hoping to change the subject so my mind won't keep thinking about his body. "What did you have in mind for tonight?"

"Well," he tells me as he opens the front gate, allowing me to pass onto the sidewalk first. It's a small, chivalrous act, but it's an act that most men my age no longer do. "I was thinking we could walk around a little, get to know each other. Then see where we end up."

That's a first.

"You just want to walk around?" I ask him, kind of surprised that was what he planned.

"I know," he admits, "it sounds weird, but sometimes I find restaurants have too many distractions. Loud televisions, loud people, it's hard to focus on what someone's saying. It's hard to really listen."

There are always these moments, I find, when I can't decide whether someone is so genuinely real that they amaze me, or if someone is so genuinely full of shit that I'm disappointed. Standing on the corner, waiting for the "do not walk" sign to change, I can't help but try to figure out which one is true for Mason. There are always people who believe that women love the romance, the kindness, the comfort from a man, so they act that way in order to convince them that's who they truly are. Slowly, over time, that front gets too hard to maintain, so they slither back to their old ways, their old habits.

It's an act and I can't decide if this is an act or not.

There's only one way to find out.

"Are you for real?" I ask him; a little too much Bronx attitude comes through in my words. "I'm sorry, I can't tell whether you're being serious or not."

He looks at me, disappointed, and takes a deep breath. The walking sign appears, but he doesn't move.

"Look," he says, looking away from me as if he's embarrassed, "I going to be completely upfront with you."

People brush past us, as the countdown to cross inches closer to zero. I find myself mesmerized, hanging on every word he's about to say.

"I've done the whole 'dating around' game," he tells me. It's a sentence that most men use as a way to brag, a badge of honor. It's an "I'm pretty desired" type of move. With him, however, he says it with a hint of disappointment, dissatisfaction.

"I'm not looking to keep playing games," he continues, "I'm tired of wasting my time on people who aren't being real. I only want to focus my time on finding something that has the potential to last. If this isn't something you really want, please don't waste my time. I will graciously walk you back to your house, no anger or animosity at all. I'm sorry, I just need you to know, I don't want to waste time with games."

Damn.

That's the first time I've ever heard those words come out of a man's mouth. Most men, especially nowadays, live and breathe by the game. If this is a game, he's damn good at it, and I won't lie, I'm curious to see what else he's got. On the other hand, if he's genuine, this could be something to fight for.

"I am so sorry," I mutter out, embarrassed. "I have a tendency to misjudge you, frequently, but tonight, there will be no games. You will get me and only me."

He smiles. "I was really hoping you'd say that. I promise, everything I do or say is who I am and what I believe. At the end of the night, if you aren't interested in that, we can go our separate ways."

"Deal," I smile back.

The "walk" sign reappears and together we cross, slowly strolling along the Brooklyn sidewalk, past the elegant brownstones, the noise of the city drowned out by our conversation. As we walk, I find myself wishing and praying that I had the power to pause time, so our effortless conversation never has to end.

"How about 20 questions?" I ask.

"Only if you go first," he responds, quickly stepping out of the way of a jogger.

Without missing a beat, I ask away.

"Full name?"

"Mason Robert Bracher."

"Oh, Robert. Not what I was expecting," I reply. "I think I was picturing something a little more Irish, like Patrick, or Liam."

"It's my father's name," he says.

"You don't seem very happy about that."

He smiles. "Is that a question?"

"Why don't you like your middle name?" I rephrase.

"It's a constant reminder that no matter how hard I try; I can never outrun our similarities."

There's a silence that falls between us, mostly my fault because I don't know what else to say. Thankfully, he seems prepared to reroute the conversation. "My turn," he tells me. "Full name."

"That's cheap, stealing my question, but I'll allow it this once. Alexandra Mary Rojas and before you waste the question on my middle name, my mother is a hardcore Catholic."

"Interesting. Are you a hardcore Catholic?" he asks.

"Wow, jumping right into those difficult questions," I laugh at him. "Religion on the first date?"

"I mean, we said no games, right?"

"Yes, we did. Well...I guess in terms of religion; I'd say I'm more spiritual." I pause to try and gather my thoughts. It isn't a topic I'm used to explaining to dates. "I believe that parts of our lives are out of our control. We have a destiny and everything that happens along the way is just getting us closer to it. I can't say I believe in something like that, but not believe in a God."

"You didn't say you were Catholic," he reminds me.

"I hate to be this stereotypical millennial, but organized religion makes no sense to me. A God I believe in doesn't require me to tell my deepest darkest secrets to a priest. The God I believe in already knows. Organized religion is just a way to attempt to brainwash people to give money and fight for a cause. Think about the Crusades. It was just a religion convincing people that they were better than others. I mean, they just..."

I quickly realize I'm rambling and stop speaking.

"Why do you do that?" he asks me.

"Do what?"

"Why do you stop speaking so suddenly, like you're afraid the person you're speaking to thinks you're crazy?"

I laugh. "Probably because most people I speak to do think I'm crazy."

He reaches out his hand, palm open, as he turns to look at me and without a second thought, I put my hand in his, our fingers locked together. Walking along the East River, the Manhattan skyline lighting up the night, I can feel the warmth from his body as we move closer together. The questions continue as he tells me about his life, his Ivy League degree, and his family. I sense the pain behind his words as he talks about his past, but he holds nothing back. Admiring his honesty, I tell him about my family, the Bronx, and my hatred toward the injustices of the world. For the first time, I have this feeling that someone is listening—like truly listening to each and every word—as I babble on about the contents of my heart.

"Most people I meet don't seem to have any idea what is going on in the world," he tells me, impressed by my passion. "I probably could do a better job keeping up, myself."

"I've seen the look on people's faces when I show up to parties. They look at me like they're afraid I'm going to go off on them about some animal-tested lipstick or non-organic alcohol."

"Wait," he interrupts, "do they actually have that? Organic beer?"

I laugh. "I don't actually know, but if not, it's a genius idea. My point is, parties aren't exactly my scene. I just feel there are better ways to spend your time, better ways to socialize."

"Well, you had me convinced they were. The way you navigated that keg stand," he tells me with a smile.

"Don't get me wrong, they used to be," I confess. "But I grew up at some point."

"Am I allowed to ask more intimate, personal questions?" he inquires. "Are we at that point in the walk yet?"

I nod.

"Who was it?" he asks.

"Who was what?" I respond, confused by his question.

"The person who made you doubt everyone's honesty, made you question everyone's integrity."

He wasn't lying. It is a personal question, one that I've never been asked before, and one that I'm not sure I've ever answered.

"I'm assuming it was my ex-boyfriend," I confess to him, not really sure of the answer myself. "We were high school sweethearts. Born and raised in the Bronx, we both had families who immigrated here. His were from El Salvador, mine are from Mexico. We lived two houses away and everyone

51

wanted us to stay together forever. My abuela would tell me every time she saw us together that our love for each other would carry us through a lifetime together."

"So, what happened?" he asks.

"Life happened," I admit. "My family didn't have much, both of my parents have a high school education, my grandparents didn't even finish high school. Growing up, I knew how hard they worked just to keep food on the table, just to keep paying the bills. Don't get me wrong, we weren't poor; we had so much, but that doesn't mean they had the privilege to work any easier. My dad worked two jobs some nights, getting no sleep between shifts. I barely saw him some days and I knew I didn't want that life for myself. When I got my scholarship to college, we all knew I had to go. Well, everyone except for my ex. He wanted to get married, to have a family, to live out our lives in the Bronx just like our families."

"And you?" he questions.

"I felt like I was meant for more. I don't know how to explain it, but deep down, I have this feeling like I am meant to do something with this life. I feel arrogant for even saying it, but I don't mean it as if I'm special. I just believe I have to do something with my life that's fulfilling, meaningful. Having a family is something I will always want, but it isn't all that I want. I'm meant to do more. So, I left, partially hoping one day we'd find our way back to each other."

I can feel his hand slipping away as I mutter those last words, so I hold on tighter, determined to make him understand this last part.

"I went back home after college," I tell him, "and realized how wrong we were for each other. By the time I graduated from college, he had already gotten married and had a child on the way. See, he didn't love me, after all that time. He loved the idea of me. He loved the idea of an intelligent, beautiful woman, dedicating her life to him and his needs. That was what he needed. That is what he hoped I would become."

"And that isn't what you want," he says.

"No. Never," I admit to him. "I want to be a wife, I want to be a mother, but I don't want to be just that. A relationship is a partnership and he just saw me as a step stool to reach his own goals."

"I'm sorry you had to learn that the hard way," he tells me. "But if I'm being honest…I'm kind of glad."

"And why's that?" I ask.

"Well, if he wasn't such an idiot, then we wouldn't be standing here right now." I feel his grip get tighter, as he turns to smile at me.

"OK, OK," I laugh, "now it's my turn. The girl from the party, I watched her hug you, like really hug you. She seemed interested."

He smiles, "You mean Sarah." He doesn't keep talking; he just stops and stares ahead.

"Oh, c'mon," I nudge him, "you can't stop now."

"There are just some people who don't bring out the best in you," he tells me. "She was one of those people."

"That's a cop-out," I tell him. "There's more to that story."

"Yes, we dated for about four months. Over that time, I didn't feel like she pushed me, or made me a better person. We had fun, she was a nice person, but I never felt…a deeper connection. I needed more than fun." As he finished speaking, there was a level of understanding we had toward each other that didn't exist earlier in the night. Out of everything he said to me, wanting a deeper connection was the most exciting of them all.

"Enough about me," he blurts out. "Your job. Tell me about your job."

"You're going to think it's crazy," I warn him.

"Try me," he says with a smile.

"I work for a company called H2O. It's a company that works to bring clean water to developing countries around the world. I work on the logistics, like deciding where we should go, and making sure the employees who go there get the job done."

"Doesn't sound crazy to me," he replies. "Do you like it?"

"I love it. It's my passion," I tell him. "Growing up, I never wanted to wake up in the morning and go to a job just to work. I wanted to do something I loved and I love this."

"That's awesome, that you found something that makes you so happy," he tells me. He's genuine when he says it, but I get the sense he doesn't feel the same.

"What about you?" I ask. "What do you do?"

"Public relations," he tells me. "I'm a PR Assistant for a small company."

"Do you like it?" I ask.

"It's a job," he says with a laugh.

I stop, pulling him back to face me.

"What's your passion?" I ask him staring into his beautiful blue eyes.

"Oh, boy," he says, looking around awkwardly. "Uhh, I guess I'd have to go with Karaoke."

"Wait, what?" I ask confused.

"Karaoke. It's a Japanese phrase that means empty orchestra," he informs me.

"No, I know what it means," I playfully slap him on the arm. "Are you serious?"

"Dead serious. It's a hidden talent of mine. I'm very popular among the drunk crowds."

"All right, then," I say to him. "Prove it."

He laughs and points to the surroundings around us.

"We are in the middle of the sidewalk," he reminds me. "You can't just do Karaoke in the middle of the sidewalk."

I grab him by the shoulders and turn him around, pointing to the sign in the building across the street. In neon letters, it simply reads "Karaoke."

"We're in Brooklyn," I remind him. "There are more Karaoke bars than people in this city."

"Pretty sure that's an inaccurate statement," he says.

"Oh shut it," I tell him, pushing him across the street and into the bar.

Multiple drinks later, Mason Robert Bracher walks off the stage a hero. The crowd of drunken people still cheer for an encore, giving high fives, slaps on the back, and even some kisses on his forehead. He makes his way up to me, with an "I told you so" smile on his face.

"Well?" he asks.

"That was the second-best rendition of Tiny Dancer I have ever heard in my life," I mention while hugging him tightly.

"Second best?" he asks, insulted.

"Yeah, second to Elton John himself," I whisper in his ear, still holding him tight. I find myself afraid to let go, like letting go would mean losing him.

He pulls back, his hands still on my hips, and stares into my eyes. Looking up at him, I feel my legs begin to go weak. I place my hands on his face, and finally behind his head. Playing with his hair, I bite my lip and look down, fearful of the urge to kiss him.

"Alex!" I hear someone call out from a few feet away. We quickly let go of each other as I see a short Asian woman pushing her way through the crowd toward us.

"Wendy!" I call out, grabbing Mason's hand and bringing him toward her.

"I can't believe you are here!" she tells me as we hug. "I would have never expected to run into you this late!"

"Well," I motion toward Mason who's standing behind me, "it's a special occasion."

"Oh my god, I'm sorry," Wendy says, quickly checking her black, pixie-cut hair as she gushes at Mason. "Hi, I'm Wendy," she offers her hand to Mason with a smile, "and you were a complete rock star up there."

Mason laughs, slightly embarrassed. "It's really nice to meet you. I kind of assumed we'd never see anyone in this bar ever again, so now I feel slightly embarrassed."

"Don't be ashamed," Wendy told him. "If I were you, I'd want everyone to remember me!"

"Who are you here with?" I ask Wendy.

"My boyfriend and a few of my friends are in the back," she tells us. "Are you guys staying? Do you want to join us?"

I look back at Mason and only want to be alone with him.

"I actually think we're going to head out," I tell her. "But it was great seeing you!" We hug goodbye and begin to head toward the door. Mason grabs my hand as we start to push through the crowd.

"Oh, wait!" Wendy calls out to us, pushing her way back for one more hug. "I forgot you aren't going to be back at work on Monday! If I don't see you, have fun in Nairobi! See you in May!"

I release Wendy from the hug as she rushes back toward her friends. With a giant pit in my stomach, I turn around and see Mason's face. All he does is stare at me, a terrible singer screaming Backstreet Boys in the background. Then, he turns to walk out the door.

As we make our way back toward the front of my house, I find myself panicking about what will happen next. The silence between us is awkwardly apparent, at least to me, and it makes me wonder whether I had just ruined a perfectly good night. We pause, outside the gate, and I try to make eye contact with him, but he continues to stare off into the distance.

"When were you going to tell me?" Mason asks.

I sigh, "I don't know, but I was going to tell you."

"We stood there and agreed," he reminds me. "No games. I told you I wasn't looking for something part-time."

"I know," I confess, "I panicked. I've never met anyone like you before and I'm willing to bet I won't meet anyone like you again. I wasn't entirely honest with you, earlier tonight. I will admit that, but after we started talking, I got afraid to tell you. Part of me wished it wasn't true and the other part knew that telling you was going to end the night. No, I don't want to play games. I like you, really like you, which is why you deserve to know the truth."

There is a lingering silence as he continues to stare into my eyes. I can tell he is hanging on my last words, worried where they are going to take us. I'd be lying if I said I wasn't worried about where they'd take us either.

"In a few days, I'm going to be moving to Nairobi for six months. There's an office opening up over there and my boss is sending me there to make sure things go smoothly."

"I wish you would have been honest with me, from the start," he tells me.

"I know. I really messed that up. I'll admit that, but I need to do this, Mason. This work is important to me and I was afraid if I told you, you would try and convince me to stay."

He sighs. "What did you see from me tonight that would even make you think I'd try to ask you to stay?"

"Nothing," I admit, "but I've been with men before who have only held me back. I was afraid you would do the same. There's a purpose I need to fulfill. Six months is a long time, and you deserve someone you don't have to wait for."

He breaks the stare for the first time. Now, instead of looking into my eyes, he is staring at the ground. "Well, I appreciate your honesty," he tells me, as a drunken group of college girls walk past having an obnoxiously loud conversation. I find my blood boiling over their incessantly annoying behavior, but Mason just stands there, straight-faced, calm as can be. It's at this moment I truly get a glimpse of the selflessness this man possesses. Here I am, standing in from of him admitting that I lied and all he can say back is that he appreciates my honesty.

"Meeting you," I tell him, "has been…so special. This was the most fun I've ever had on a date."

I can feel the tears begin to form as I struggle to hold it together. I put my hand to his cheek, lifting up his face to make eye contact with him. "You are truly one of a kind," I tell him, unable to keep from crying. "I will never forget meeting you."

I let go of his face and rush into the house, afraid to let him see the tears pouring down my face. I leave him there, standing in front of my house, in the November night, heartbroken.

———————

Up before the sun the next morning, I find myself sitting in the park, on my favorite bench. The cool, winter breeze signals a stark contrast in temperature from the night before as I wrap myself in my fleece blanket. I lay down on the wooden bench, staring up at the sky, disappointed by the cards life has dealt me. Watching the morning light begin to spread across the sky, I can't help but think about Mason. The authenticity with which he lives his life, the heart that he holds in his chest, the strength hiding in his arms, and I can still feel the pieces of my heart inside my chest.

"That was the seventh time."

I'm startled back to reality by the sound of a voice as it cuts through the early morning silence. There, standing in the distance, leaning against a tree, is Mason and in his hands, he holds two coffee cups.

"May I?" he asks, walking toward me and gesturing to the space on the bench next to me. I nod as he sits and hands me the coffee. A sense of calm lingers in the air between us as I offer to wrap my blanket around him.

"The seventh time?" I ask him, confused by his statement.

"You've been misjudging me a lot," he reminds me, "and yesterday, you ended our night misjudging me again."

"I'm sorry if I offended you," I apologize.

"You didn't offend me," he informs me, "you misjudged me."

"How did I do that?" I ask.

He turns to look at me, puts his coffee cup down on the ground, and grabs both of my hands. "Look, I can't say I wasn't surprised last night. I was very surprised, but I can't just let you go to Kenya without being honest with you. As long as you are with me, I am never going to hold you back from fulfilling your purpose. You, however, cannot hold me back from fulfilling mine."

"I'm pretty sure I let you sing your heart out last night, so I haven't been holding you back," I remind him with a laugh.

"I'm talking about my other purpose," he says.

"Oh, I wasn't aware there was a second one," I tell him.

"I believe it's you," he replies.

"Me?"

"I believe my purpose in life is to spend as much time with you as I possibly can. I believe I met you for a reason and I'm not willing to let you disappear without knowing what that reason may be. I want to be with you, whether you are here or in Kenya, I will be here waiting."

With those last words, I feel his hands brush across my face. I take mine, place them behind his head and begin to play with his hair again.

"I can't kiss you," I inform him, staring into his eyes.

"And why's that?" he asks.

"I told Dylan I'd only kiss you if I thought you might be the one."

"Well then," he says, closing his eyes, "tell me you don't think I may be the one."

Closer and closer I move, knowing the words won't come out of my mouth. I stop; our lips about to touch, and I close my eyes. Finally, I lean in, our lips touch and the pieces inside my chest suddenly feel connected.

They suddenly feel complete.
They suddenly feel like one.

Chapter 5
May 12th, 2011

Sitting there, watching him dance throughout the kitchen to some Rihanna song I've never heard of before, I suddenly can't help but feel this overwhelming sense of joy. It started the second I exited to the terminal and saw him standing there, a box of Reese's peanut butter cups in his left hand, a box of pizza in his right, and a smile that lit up the terminal. Crowds of people moved past me in each direction, some eagerly running toward their loves, others sobbing as they slowly moved away to catch their flights. Dylan hovered over the corner of Mason's shoulder, her head down and eyes locked into her phone. His eyes, though, were only looking for me. His gorgeous blue eyes, with his perfectly sculpted hair, made him look better than I remembered and much better than the poor-quality FaceTime made him look. Meanwhile, I exited the plane in yoga pants and a sweatshirt with my hair tied up in a sloppy ponytail. Yet for some reason, the way he looked at me made me feel like I was the only person in the entire airport.

When Dylan finally looked up from her phone, realizing I was mere feet away, she squealed and jumped with joy. Even as she squeezed me tight, all I could do was look at Mason. I found myself preparing for the satisfaction of his touch. I gently pushed Dylan away once I realized she had started sobbing for joy, knowing that she wasn't going to stop, and walked up to Mason.

"Everyone kept telling me to get flowers, but I knew exactly what you really needed," he told me, handing me the Reese's and box of pizza.

Without even looking, I turned and shoved them into Dylan's arms, never once breaking contact with Mason's eyes. I felt my smile widen, as he got closer, finally placing his hand on my back, and kissing me.

It made me feel unequivocally happy.

It's the type of happiness that quickly envelops your body, wrapping itself around every inch of your body, sending these warm, tingling chills down your spine.

It's the type of happiness that, hours later, I can still feel in my fingertips and all the way down to my toes, but most importantly, it makes my heart feel more complete than it's ever felt before. Especially now, sitting in his kitchen, as the trapezius muscle in his back becomes more defined with each move he makes, displaying a perfect V-shape from his shoulders down to his waist. They flex underneath his t-shirt and 'Top Chef' apron as he moves some pots and pans around the kitchen. The sight of those muscles gives me desires I haven't thought about in a long time…desires I almost forgot existed. Then suddenly, like an alarm detecting an uninvited intruder, my brain catches up with the warmth that has completely seized my body. The darkness starts to spread from my brain, traveling with lightning speed to the far corners of my body, turning my warm chills into freezing cold shock. Now, looking at him, all I see is doubt.

He won't stay with you.

He doesn't want you the way you want him.

He's just being nice.

You don't think he's waited around for you all these months, do you?

Like an unhinged train, the thoughts keep going and going, refusing to stop no matter how badly I try. The seeds have already been planted, and it takes all the joy away, turning it into sickening anxiety. As he continues to make his way around the kitchen, I suddenly realize I don't know him. I begin to think about the fact that the relationship we have isn't real. It's been a one-week courtship followed by six months of phone calls and FaceTime sessions. You can't build a relationship off of that. I'm scared to realize that I don't actually know the man standing in front of me, but I can't shake the feeling that deep down, I do. At least, I feel like that's all I want to do; know him. Deep down, I just want to be with him.

That's when my legs step into action. Listening to the alarm bells going off in my brain, I stand up at the table looking at him. "Mason," I say softly, but he doesn't hear me over his incessant singing. "Mason!" I say much louder now, almost aggressively.

He turns to look at me, this boyish smile on his face, and I realize it's that look, those eyes, that scare me the most.

"I have to go," I say, grabbing my bag off the back of the chair and walking toward the front door. I walk past Kevin, sitting on the couch watching some stupid comedy movie with a giant bowl of popcorn on his lap. He tosses the popcorn into his mouth as I walk past the television, his head smoothly moving around the shape of my body to not miss a second of his precious movie.

"Alex," I hear Mason call after me from the kitchen. "Alex, wait!"

I hesitate. I don't know why, but for a second, I stop, waiting for him. Then I feel him reaching for me as his hand grabs mine. I pull mine away and turn to him.

"What do you want?" I say to him, a sense of anger in my tone. It wasn't said the way I intended, but my fear is in control now. "What do you want?"

A look of shock takes over his face, and I realize it's the first time I've yelled at him since we met. "I'm sorry," he responds softly. "Did I say something wrong?"

Of course not. Why would he ever say something that bothers me or makes me mad? That's the problem with him; it always feels too good to be true.

"Is there something I did?" he questions me, as I watch Kevin out of the side of my eye throw a few more cornels of popcorn into his mouth, his eyes no longer fixed on the television, but now focused squarely on us.

"I just can't do this, Mason," I confess to him, the anxiety and fear making me feel on edge. "I just can't do this!"

"OK," he says calmly, still speaking much softer than I am. "OK. Let's talk about it then."

"I don't want to talk about it!" I yell at him, throwing my hands in the air because he doesn't get it. "I'm just going to go!" I turn to walk away.

"I just don't understand what I did!" This time he begs, begs for an answer.

"You just don't get it!" I turn back pointing at him. "You haven't done anything! This," I motion to him standing there in the apron, "this isn't real, Mason. This is all just an act. No one does this, not these days. What guy these days knows how to cook?"

He stands there silently, thinking that I'm going to continue my rant, and then quickly answers when he realizes I'm waiting for a response.

"Oh, uhh, I don't know. I guess people who need to eat. They know how to cook," he says sarcastically. "I learned when I was growing up, ya know, when my mom stopped taking care of my family."

I feel a pang of guilt in my gut, but I'm determined that he won't use his sad childhood to win this battle. "And Rihanna? When did men start dancing around the kitchen to Rihanna?" I accuse him.

"Are you serious right now?" he asks me. "Because I'm a man I can't listen to Rihanna? Kevin," he turns to Kevin, who's still watching our argument like it's the best drama on TV, "when did I start listening to Rihanna?"

Kevin throws another piece of popcorn into his mouth. "I think it was about the same time you got your first period," he says, laughing.

"Oh, real great, Kevin," I snap back at him as he starts choking on the popcorn from laughing so hard. "Way to bring your sexist remarks into the conversation. They really help."

Kevin just gives a thumb up and smiles, but Mason's eyes are back on me. The look on his face, the one of remorse, changes to one of disappointment. "Don't attack his sexist remarks when you're the one accusing me of not being real. I don't get what you want me to do, Alex. Do you want me to treat you like shit? Would that make you feel better? Better yet, how about I sit on my ass and watch some football while you cook me a nice meal? Huh? How do you like that?"

I go to reply, but there's no stopping him now. "You sit here and pretend like you care about equality, yet you stand on the outside of the world and put all men into this box. You've been putting me in that box since the day we met. You believe I'm supposed to act a certain way. You question everything I do, and how have I responded? I've continued to be the man I am. I've continued to prove myself to you for the past seven months. This is me, so what are you so afraid of?"

I stand there, staring at him. Kevin's no longer eating but is now just staring at us, open-mouthed. I want to reply, but I just can't find the words to say.

"What are you afraid of, Alex?" he says again forcefully, but no reply comes to my mind.

"What…"

Jumping onto him, I wrap my legs around his waist. My hands pull his face to me, as I feel his chapped lips against mine. The warmth returns, now as a burning desire erasing the fear and anxiety from earlier, as it spreads like wildfire throughout my body. I find myself wanting him more than I've ever wanted another man before, and my body trembles as I feel his hands move along my lower back.

Kevin clears his throat, trying to remind us that another person is in the room, and I flip him off before putting my hands back into Mason's hair. As he carries me into the bedroom, closing the door behind him, he lays me down on the bed, climbing on top of me. My hands, slipping underneath his shirt, move along the groves of his hips, feeling the ridges of his abdominal muscles, counting each and every one. I pause above his chest, brushing the wispy chest hair beneath my fingers, and feeling his heart pounding rapidly. He moves gently, unhooking the button on my pants and slowly sliding his hand down below my waist. I close my eyes, reveling from the sensation of his touch.

The longer I lay there, the greater the sensation becomes, sending burning waves of desire to the far corners of my body. I suddenly find myself wanting him, no needing him, right this very second. The tortured months of buildup, the years of waiting for a romance like this, and now the reward for my patience makes me quiver. Kissing his neck, feeling his deep breaths on my cheek, I pull him toward me, no longer worried about the doubts of before, but simply letting our instincts take over.

Hours later a closing door from the hallway wakes me up, my body still tingling with satisfaction. The last remaining light from the setting sun makes its way through the window, casting a shadow on the clothes piled on the floor. I can't help but stare at the man laying here next to me, and I watch his chest rise and fall with each breath as I tenderly brush my hand through his hair. Feeling his damp sweat between my fingers brings my mind back to before, and the feeling of his sweat dripping onto my naked body. I trace my hand down to his cheek, feeling his light stubble brush against my palm and finally let my hand rest on his chest, perfectly contoured to fit the shape of my hand. His heart has slowed from before, now beating steadily with each breath he takes.

It is at this moment, in the aftermath of our passion, that I truly understand the origin of my fear. The truth is hard to accept but impossible to ignore.

I want him with every inch of my body and every corner of my heart. I want him like nothing I've ever wanted before, and the truth is; I'm afraid to ever let go.

Chapter 6
Session 2

I've always thought of the act of meditation as a phenomenal concept. A person who successfully meditates needs the ability to focus on two factors at the same time. The first factor is the noise around them. Most people meditate in the silence of their own homes, making this factor insignificant. A true meditator, however—one who has mastered the art of meditation—can meditate anywhere. A park, the subway, the middle of traffic, it doesn't matter where. A true meditator can create silence from the noise around.

The second factor is even harder than the first. Not only do successful meditators need to create silence from the noise around them, but they also need to silence the one part of our body that never stops churning.

The brain.

Think about that.

The brain, which allows us to think, to create a concept like meditation, gets ignored, silenced. The one thing that helps us feel, move, talk, and live, gets completely silenced for an extended period of time. By doing this, people who meditate often identify as having less stress, worry, anxiety, and have an overall higher sense of happiness.

It's a really fascinating concept if you think about it. If meditation truly creates these stress-free, happier people, why doesn't everyone do it?

Silence.

With the invention of headphones, speakers, iPhones, silence has changed, evolved, and diminished over the course of the last few decades. Sure, maybe long ago, silence was much more common, but today, people are constantly listening to music, podcasts, talking to friends. There is no silence. People don't even fall asleep with silence anymore, with televisions being turned on all night, or noise machines being used as sleep aids.

Some people even fear silence.

Silence provides us the opportunity to self-reflect, to become more self-aware, to be in touch with our feelings. That sounds great, if becoming more self-aware doesn't scare you, or if being in touch with your feelings doesn't create more anxiety. The truth is, most people know what lies deep within. It isn't that they are unaware of the secrets they hide; it's just that they choose to cover them up, hoping no one will ever find them. A secret is like a giant hole in the ground covered with leaves. The person who dug the hole and covered it with leaves knows it's there, but no one else does. When that person keeps busy, welcomes the noises and distractions of life, the fact that there's a hole in the ground moves toward the back of the mind. It never disappears but is thought about less frequently. There are simply more distractions to focus on than the hole.

When there aren't the noises of life, however, there are no distractions. Now, the person can only think about the hole, and the fact that the hole is there becomes the only thought on the mind. The silence makes it impossible to disappear.

I'm not used to a ton of silence.

It makes me aware of the giant leaf-covered hole.

That is why sitting here, awkwardly staring around Dr. McKnight's small home, the silence is killing me. Out of the corner of my eye, I can see her staring at me, but avoiding eye contact is my only goal at the moment. If I make eye contact, it just makes the silence more awkward, so I find things around the room to look at; the black spiral staircase in the far corner of the room that leads upstairs, the long, rectangle, dining room table that easily seats eight people, even the photos on the wall of McKnight with two young boys seemingly standing in the same place year after year in each picture. I notice the owl, its eyes open with its wings beginning to spread while it still rests, two feet securely on the branch, sitting on the table next to me.

I would not be able to meditate.

The silence makes my brain work overtime.

Finally, after what feels like hours, but I know is only a matter of minutes, McKnight decides to break the silence.

"You seem uncomfortable," she points out, like I didn't know that already. To be honest, I don't even know how to sit down without looking uncomfortable. Everything about being here makes me uncomfortable. The silence just makes it worse, and I question how one even responds to a statement like that. I can continue to sit here in silence and ignore her, or I can find something to say back. Both options just seem to make this situation more awkward. Only one option, however, will break this painful silence.

"I thought the whole point of these sessions was for us to talk?" I ask her, as a simple reminder that she isn't exactly doing her job well. I can feel myself getting frustrated with this wasted time.

"It can be," she tells me. "It also can be a place for people to reflect, to think, to process."

"You're telling me, you get paid to sit here and watch people think?" I ask her in disbelief. "That sounds like an easy job."

I know the last part was unnecessary. Normally, I wouldn't fathom making an insulting comment like that, but the silence has me angry, frustrated. She also just sits there so calm, so composed, that I find myself getting even angrier with her. It's like she knows my time is being wasted, but she doesn't care.

"Some people simply need a thought partner, someone who is there on their journey but doesn't dictate which direction they go. They have the ability to think, to reflect, and to process their emotions and thoughts," she says, without a hint of anger at my comment. Smooth and steady, she continues, "Others need someone to do that with them, to guide them. They need more help working through their thoughts, or their feelings."

"Which one am I?" I ask smugly. Although the truth is that deep down, I'm wildly curious about the answer.

"Which one do you think you are?" she replies back.

My least favorite game.

I sigh heavily, place my hands above my head, and close my eyes. God, I wish I could have a cigarette right now. Everything about this woman makes me want to smoke. "I don't really understand why you have to avoid answers to questions. You aren't a politician. Just answer the question. Which one am I?"

Again, it comes out as impolite, impatient. It isn't my intent to insult her, but it also isn't my intent to waste my time playing these mind games. She pauses, smiles, still not impacted by my rudeness, and then she begins, "A question is a powerful tool."

I roll my eyes and put my head down, in disbelief that this is how I'm forced to spend my time.

"A question," she continues, immune to my excessive reaction, "opens up possibilities. It gets people thinking, helps them reflect. A question guides people toward an answer, whether right or wrong. A question doesn't give the answer."

"Why can't you just give me the answer?" I ask again, ignoring her attempt at some wise comment. "You seem to think you have the answers to everything."

"Why do you insist on me giving you one?" she asks me back.

The silence comes back, but this time it's my fault. I find myself in such disbelief, such frustration at the direction of the conversation and the fact that she continues to play this game. I look out the window, at the rain droplets collecting and steaming their way from the top of the white window frame to the bottom.

"Mason, look," she begins, with the tone of someone who isn't trying to yield power, but trying to open a conversation, "I do not sit here as the one with all the answers. You have the answers. I can sit here all day and tell you what I would do, but that doesn't help you. You don't need my opinion or advice. You need your own."

I sit there and watch as she explains her answer to me. My heart can be felt pounding beneath my chest and I notice my fists clenched tightly between my legs. Taking a deep breath, I slowly unclench my fists, hoping she won't see my physical reaction to the conversation.

Of course, she misses nothing.

"I know that that answer upsets you," she continues, gesturing to my hands. "It might not make sense now, but it will…one day." Then she's silent again. This time it's on purpose, giving my body a chance to calm down. I feel my heart begin to slow and the heat dissipate from my face as McKnight starts the conversation back up, "Why do you believe the silence is so frustrating for you?"

I respond, but this time with a composed tone, "I like to keep busy."

It's partially the truth. I do like to keep busy. The real truth, though, isn't something she needs to know. I hate where the silence takes me. Unfortunately, my answer doesn't seem sufficient enough, judging by McKnight's continual silence and incessant staring, so I continue my answer.

"I told you last time, I don't like wasting my time. I only have so much time to get everything done that I need. Sitting around in silence is just time wasted. It's time that I could be spending taking care of my responsibilities."

"Do you feel like you have a lot of responsibilities?" she asks me curiously, completely changing the subject. It's another infuriating trick of hers, this ability to take one word in one sentence and then drag it out to mean something entirely off-topic.

"C'mon," I beg, "don't do that. Everyone has responsibilities. Those two boys probably don't take care of themselves." I'm pointing up at the photograph on the wall.

She seems taken aback by the statement like it was one she didn't expect. I sense a slight change in her facial expression before she catches herself and smiles. It isn't what I intended to say, but my frustration was unable to be contained. That's a fact she quickly picks up on.

"You're right," she says.

"Right about what?" I ask.

"The boys didn't take care of themselves," she tells me. "I took care of them for a very, very long time. It felt like a lot of responsibility at the time. I'm not afraid to admit that some days, that responsibility felt like a burden and some days, it felt like a blessing. That doesn't make me a bad mother."

"Oh," I reply slowly, unsure how I'm expected to respond. This is the first time she's ever spoken about herself or her family. "I'm…uhh…sorry."

"Oh, please don't be," she tells me. "It's the joys of being a parent. Your responsibilities create the foundation for a good life."

I nod as my guilt builds up, forcing me to speak. "Yeah…sometimes my responsibilities can feel like a burden, but I always make sure I get them done," I tell her, finding it easier to be honest than I imagined.

"I'm sure the people in your life appreciate that about you. How do you think they would describe you, Mason?" she asks gently. "Like if we asked your family or friends to tell us about you?"

"How would they describe me?" I ask back, as if it's an unbelievably stupid question. The truth is, though, I don't actually think I know the answer. It's not like I've gone around and asked my family or friends to tell me about myself. I can't imagine many people have.

She smiles and adjusts her body in the chair in a way that sends a clear message; she's getting comfortable and has no problem with my silence.

Seeing as the silence doesn't suit me, I'll try to answer her question. "Well…I think they'd say I'm a helpful, responsible person," I reply, very matter-of-factly. Thinking about it, I don't think they'd stay around if I weren't a helpful or responsible person. It seems like the truth, but I realize it sounds like the answer a second grader would give to a teacher.

"Would you agree with them?" she questions back as she crosses her arms in front of her.

"What type of question is that?" I reply hastily. "Of course I'd agree with them. I work very hard supporting my friends and family when they need me."

She pauses for a second, pondering her next question. I'm not entirely sure if she pauses because she doesn't know what she's going to ask next, or simply for dramatic effect. "Were they surprised then, to hear about your incident in the supermarket?"

Definitely a pause for dramatic effect. She knew that question was coming before I even walked in the door this morning. I fell right into her trap, once again. Now I'm pausing. I'm pausing out of disbelief, I'm pausing out of anger, and I'm pausing because I have no idea how to answer the question. I also have no desire to answer the question.

"I'd rather not talk about that," I admit to her. "It's over and done with."

She laughs, "Well, according to this court order I have to sign, I'd say it's pretty important. I'd also mention that it requires us to speak about it."

I'm quickly reminded that this woman won't take my bullshit.

"So once again," she continues, "how did your friends and family—the people you say think of you as responsible and helpful—react when they heard about your incident?"

I decide to go with the truth. It doesn't seem like there's any better option anymore. "They were surprised," I admit.

"Surprised?" she asks with sass in her voice. "I'm surprised when I find a dollar on the street or when someone throws me an unexpected party for my birthday. How did they really—"

"Shocked," I firmly tell her, cutting her off before she got the chance to finish the question. "They felt shocked."

"Why?" she asks back quickly. "What shocked them?"

It's like she has a rope, and she's standing at the bottom of my leaf-covered hole with the rope tied around my ankle. With each question, with each session, she's pulling harder and faster. I'm trying to resist, but she has this brute strength and unrelenting resolve that continues to win out.

"Of course they felt shocked," I decide to respond with some attitude, hoping it will deter her from asking any more questions. "It's not who I am."

"What part of the incident isn't who you are?" she responds. "Because usually when I'm getting to know people, I tend to judge them on their actions, the way they hold themselves. That's how I learn who a person is deep down."

"What does that even mean?" I push back. "The whole thing, everything that happened. That isn't who I am. I'm telling you that's not who I am."

She nods, "But I find that's the problem with words. People use the words they believe others want to hear, not necessarily the words that express their true character."

I slam my fist down on the table next to me. The lamp shakes as the owl falls to its side. "I just said that isn't who I am!" I exclaim.

"Hmm, interesting," she calmly replies.

"You've got to be kidding me. What is so god damn interesting about that? You think that's who I am?"

By now, my heart is thumping beneath my chest, the slight pulse evident through my long-sleeve shirt, and my face feels flushed as I feel my muscles tightening up with each passing second.

"I don't know who you are," she begins to admit. "I've only just met you. I don't have much to go on."

She pauses, but I have nothing left to say. Sitting there, she just watches me, like a scientist watches a lab rat. Observing my every move, reading my posture, my facial expression, my breaths, she takes note of it all. She lets the silence fall over the room again. This time, the only noise breaking the silence is my deep, labored breaths.

"Take a look at your hands," she tells me after enough time has passed.

I look down at my hands, my fists, balled up between my legs. As I open them, my palms are crimson red from the squeezing, and my fingers shake as I rest them on top of my knees.

"Are you shocked?" she asks me as a true, genuine look of concern covers her face. "Are you really shocked about what happened?"

Staring down at my hands, I know the truth. It's a truth I've known for a long, long time, but one I've been terribly afraid to admit. "I'm not," I admit to her.

"And why not?" she wonders.

"For the past few months, I've found myself..." I pause, unsure of the words to describe it, "...easily agitated."

"And are you typically an angry person?" she questions, a clear sense of curiosity in her voice.

"No," I reassure her confidently. "No. I'm not. That isn't who I am. I don't know what happened. One second, I'm grocery shopping and the next..."

"You've punched a man in the face," she finishes my sentence for me, sensing the difficulty in getting it out.

"In front of his kids," I shamefully admit. "He had two young kids in the cart and I still did it."

"Why?" she questions.

Isn't that the million-dollar question?

"I've just been so angry...so incredibly angry," I confess. "I went down the aisle and saw him standing in front of the baby formula. It was literally the only thing I came into the store to get. I put the very last one in my cart and walked away for a second to grab a bottle at the end of the aisle. When I turned around, this little kid was standing there, holding the formula from *my* cart. I watched him start to walk away, so I rushed over and tried to kindly explain to him that I needed it back. He refused to give it to me, so I just took it. Ripped it right out of the kid's hands, which of course made him scream bloody murder at the top of his lungs. Then this guy comes running around the aisle and sees me standing there in front of his screaming child. The kid tells him I took the formula from him, and completely leaves out the part where he took it from my cart. I had it first. It was pouring rain outside, and I needed to get home. I wasn't going to go to another store when I had the formula first. Of course, the dad got pissed, so he's yelling at me, asking me what my problem is and then, he went to grab it back from my hands. I pushed him away, because it was the first thing I could think of, and that only made him push me back, so without even thinking...I just punched him."

She lets me sit with those thoughts, as our time together begins to wind down. Then, after some time, she begins to speak. "Have you ever felt this much anger before?" she asks.

"No," I confess to her, "nothing like this. I mean, I've been angry before, but this was beyond anything I've ever experienced. It's part of the reason it happened. I know that isn't an excuse, but I'd never acted that way in the past, so how was I to know it was going to happen?"

"These past two sessions, you've seemed to get pretty easily agitated," she reminds me.

"I know," I tell her, "I used to be the calm one. Every time something happened, I would be the one constant for everyone. I had my head on straight. I would be able to defuse any conflict. Now...now, I just find myself wanting to hit people constantly. When I get cut off on the road, or someone says something rude or disrespectful, I find myself literally losing it."

"This is a new emotion for you," she tells me.

"Yeah, it's very new, at least this much of it. My mom suggested anger management classes after she found out I'd been arrested. She just kept going on and on about how this was how my father acted, so irrationally."

"How'd that feel when she said that to you?" she asks.

"It hurt...a lot. I've worked hard my entire life to be the exact opposite of my father. This moment was exactly who he was, and that anger—I'm not even surprised it's inside of me."

"Why's that?"

"It was the same anger he showed us each and every day. I always knew it was possible that it was there...resting inside me, but I also always believed I'd be in enough control to make sure it never came out."

"Here we are," she tells me, "back to this word control. You seem to believe that control can solve all of your problems."

"Control is everything," I remind her. "If I can control myself, my impulses, I can be who I need to be."

"I need you to stop thinking about who other people need you to be," she tells me. "That is what got you into this mess in the first place. You consistently believe that people need you to be in control. What do you need? That's what you need to ask yourself."

"I think I agree with my mom," I tell her. "I think I need help with anger management."

"People who need anger management classes are people whose anger is so bad, so ingrained, that they need to develop ways to cope. They practice ways

71

to handle their anger, but oftentimes acknowledge that it won't ever go away. They never learn to control their anger. That's why it's called anger management, not anger control. You, however—you don't need to know how to cope, you need to know how to talk."

I look up at her and notice this sadness that has overtaken her face. "You," she continues, "you need to talk about what's making you angry."

Deep down, I know she's right. The hole is there, but avoiding it isn't an option anymore.

"I find talking just makes me angrier," I tell her.

"For many people, it does," she reassures me. "Some people don't talk because of sadness and some don't talk because of anger. Those are the ways people cope."

"How did you cope?" I ask her. It's a question I know I shouldn't have asked. "I'm sorry. I meant no disrespect by the question. You just seem to know a lot about this, that's all. I figured you'd been through it before."

"I'm not offended by your question, Mason. It's not uncommon to want to know how others grieve. Sometimes, we use it as an example for ourselves. I will, however, push you to let go of what others do or have done. These sessions—these are for you to focus on what you need to do, not others."

I wait, hoping she'll answer the question, but she never does.

"Unfortunately, that's all the time we have for today. I truly look forward to continuing this talk next week."

She stands, which is my cue to do the same. Still caught up in her words, my head feels like a dense fog cloud, making it difficult to think. As I exit, she smiles and closes the door behind me. Instinctively, I reach into my back pocket and find the one thing I know will clear the fog. Putting the cigarette into my mouth, I light it up and begin the journey back to reality.

Chapter 7

Derrick Williams sat in the car outside the church, the bitterly cold, winter wind and the lack of motivation preventing him from going inside. The newly renovated, stone church towered in front of him, with its elegant windows reflecting the light from inside. He always found it ironic that such a beautiful structure consistently welcomed the worst that the town had to offer. Sure, the church was home to some of the greatest people he knew, seeking an opportunity to continue to become better, but it also welcomed the degenerates, the failures, and the weak, all seeking redemption and forgiveness. Unfortunately, he was one of those degenerates.

This lack of motivation, though, wasn't a new feeling; it had followed him to each meeting since the beginning. People told him it would happen. They told him he'd continue to find reasons not to go, and they reminded him it was always his choice to make. No one else could decide for him. Just like the weeks before, he took a deep breath, turned off the car, and counted backward from five.

Five.

Four.

Three.

Two.

One.

It was a technique his wife had taught him years ago, when he needed to do something, but couldn't find the desire to do it. "Just tell yourself you'll do it when you get to zero and count backward from five," she'd always say. She convinced him that if he did it over and over again for small tiny decisions, like picking a meal at a restaurant, he would develop a habit. Slowly, over time, his body actually started to respond and anytime he got to zero, it knew he had to act. It was one of those stupid ideas that completely changed his life, helped him fight the urge to drink, forced him to come to these meetings, and even led to most of his success at the law firm.

At zero, he opened the car door, stepped out into the frigid evening, and hustled his way into the church. The warmth welcomed him the second the large wooden doors closed behind him. A towering Jesus stood before him at the end of the long center aisle, as a few individuals kneeled in the pews praying. Looking away, he turned left and headed for the classrooms down the hallway from the entrance. As he approached, he could hear the sound of awkward conversations coming from the end of the hall. Opening the door, the small, crowded room materialized before him. The cold, metal chairs with the soft seat cushions were placed in an organized circle as he headed straight for the coffee. It was a routine for him, one he developed just to feel comfortable. Walk in, get some coffee because it's going to be a long night, greet the usual suspects, and take a seat in the same seat as the first day almost ten years ago. Since that day, he'd watched people walk in and out of meetings week after week ready to battle the demons inside of them.

"Attention, everyone," the group leader announced. Vicky Giraldi had been running the group since the beginning, giving up many weekday and weekend nights to be with those who needed her most. "If you could all join the circle, so we can get started with the prayer."

They stood together, hand in hand, and recited the Serenity Prayer before taking a seat. "Thank you all for joining us. I'm happy to see the room so full, especially with the impending storm, so let's not waste any time and jump right in. If anyone feels compelled to begin, please go ahead."

Derrick sat there silently, listening to story after story. The single guy who struggled to keep a relationship because of his excessive drinking, the elderly woman who used her vermouth to drown out the thought of her deceased husband, and then the room fell silent. Derrick felt a nudge on his side and turned to look at his sponsor next to him, motioning for him to speak.

"Uh, hi. My name is Derrick," he started, "and I'm an alcoholic."

"Hi, Derrick," the group replied in unison.

"I am currently nine years sober, but I'm about two months away from being ten years." Older group members nodded with a smile while a few of the newer ones perked up, impressed by his sobriety. "I guess right now I'd say it just feels like I'm going through the motions. You'd think that the longer you stay sober, the easier it becomes, but I actually find it to be the opposite. I think it becomes easier to slip up the longer you're sober." He took a deep breath, "It's like starting anything new; you're always so cautious, so careful, but when you have success, you sometimes get careless, and that can lead to mistakes."

"Have there been any mistakes lately?" the group leader probed.

"No…Not mistakes necessarily," he explained, "but definitely thoughts about making mistakes. You see, I've been struggling a lot lately with my son. He's getting older and becoming more…independent, I guess. I was exceptionally close to my first-born, and I felt like raising him and being his father was just easy. My youngest, though—each day it requires more and more work just to get through to him." Derrick paused to think for a minute as the group continued to listen intently. "I push him, a lot, probably too hard. He's just got this potential to be better than everyone around him, but he continues to try and blend in. It's like he tries to live in the shadows when he was born for the spotlight, and I just struggle to understand it because I always desired to be the best, always fought to be number one and so did my eldest. It's so hard for me to understand why he wouldn't want to stand out. That leads me to push him, which leads to him resisting, and that drives me to want to drink."

Derrick paused and took a sip of his coffee. "I love my son, with all my heart, but it pains me to think that he might see me as the enemy. I will never be perfect, but I know I can be better…especially for him."

———————

The windshield wipers moved slowly back and forth, as the snow continued to stick to the ground outside. Cars littered the streets, filled with families getting last minute supplies before the storm. Half the drivers on the road moved cautiously below the speed limit, fearful of the tiny snow covering the street ahead of them. The second half sped around them, hoping to get to the stores before the storm became worse. Dontrell fell somewhere in the middle of those two groups, as he diligently followed the speed limit heading over to Elizabeth's house. JJ's younger brother, Caleb, and two of his friends heckled each other in the backseat as Dontrell maintained two hands on the wheel and eyes on the road the entire time.

"You sure you don't want to drink tonight?" JJ asked, sitting in the front seat next to him, playing with the radio dial. "I feel like you're always the one driving. I don't mind taking a shift, so you can cut loose."

"Nah," Dontrell replied, "I'm all good. I've got practice tomorrow morning. Not to mention with the state championships coming up, I really don't want to have to worry about losing again." He appreciated the gesture. JJ was always offering to drive and making sure guys chipped in for gas money any time Dontrell drove them places.

"Yeah…I get that. Plus I can't imagine your father finding out you went to swim practice drunk," JJ responded with a laugh.

Dontrell smirked back. JJ didn't even know the half of it. All JJ saw was the over-competitive, drill sergeant Derrick Williams was at races. No one knew the former alcoholic, angry Derrick Williams that Dontrell had experienced before. Being drunk at a swim practice would piss off both versions of his father. "I don't ever want to know his reaction."

"Is he always like that?" JJ asked. "So intense?"

"Usually he is," Dontrell replied, as the car pulled up in front of Elizabeth's house. "But my mom's pretty good at bringing out his calm side. She helps ease his intensity."

The massive contemporary home was set back on the property, leaving room for a spacious front yard and a long winding driveway. "Holy shit," one of Caleb's friends replied from the back. "I didn't even know houses like this existed in this town."

JJ laughed, "That's because you spend all your time on the other side of Main Street. This house is nothing compared to some of the houses around here."

Walking out into the cold, the snow had covered enough of the ground to leave footprints behind the boys as they headed toward the front door. Dontrell and JJ walked ahead, the others laughing and giggling while throwing snow at each other; they didn't seem to mind the cold. They rounded the side of the house, following the directions Elizabeth had given them earlier in the night, and headed toward the basement door off the back porch.

Noises from the neighbor's yard caused Dontrell to look up. Standing on her back porch, preemptively throwing down salt was an older woman who stopped when she heard the noises coming from next door. She froze there, looking up at the boys as they continued to goof off in the middle of the driveway.

"Caleb! Cut it out!" JJ called out to his brother. "Hi, ma'am. We're sorry for the noise. Have a good night!" He waved at the woman as they walked down the stairs toward the basement door, his brother and friends silently and quickly catching up.

"Nice job, you idiots," JJ whispered, slapping his brother on the back of the head. "The last thing we need to do is draw unwanted attention. Just do me a favor and stay inside until we leave. Got it?"

"Got it!" the three replied back in unison, saluting JJ and quietly giggling to each other afterward.

"Like a bunch of high school girls," JJ whispered to Dontrell, opening the door to the basement and stepping out of the cold.

Elizabeth Caraveli's basement was the size of most people's homes. It sprawled the length of the house and was an entirely separate living quarters, complete with three bedrooms, a kitchen, bathroom, and living room. Most people would have rented it out, making some more income to pay the bills, but Elizabeth's parents didn't need the money. Her father, some international businessman, made more money than he knew what to do with. Everyone knew the Caravelis, especially because the family donated money to most places around town. Heck, the gym at the high school was named after them since her father paid for the renovations two y ears ago.

Seeing her guests walk in, Elizabeth jumped up from the couch and rushed to the door. She gave JJ a quick hug and introduced herself to Caleb and his friends. Finally, she turned to Dontrell; grabbing his arm and rubbing it up and down, she leaned in to whisper "hello" into his ear. She lingered there, holding him tightly, making him feel wildly uncomfortable and causing JJ to wink at him excessively.

"I'm so glad you came," she said, finally pulling away, but never breaking eye contact with Dontrell. "Heard you had a great race today. Doesn't surprise me!"

"Yeah…thanks. It went OK," Dontrell replied. "It wasn't anything too special."

"Too special?" JJ asked with a smile on his face, feeding into the fire. He placed his arm around Dontrell's neck, pulling him in. "This man set a school record, county record, and state record. All in one race! He's quite the hero, Elizabeth. Some lucky girl better scoop him up soon!"

Dontrell glared at him, "Technically, I only broke the school record, seeing as someone else currently has his name next to the other two."

Elizabeth laughed, "I know nothing about swimming, so to me it sounds like a good race! Someone get this man a drink!"

"Actually," Dontrell replied, gently removing her hand from his arm, "I'm going to go grab some snacks. I'm starving."

Before Elizabeth had a chance to continue the conversation, Dontrell was already swiftly moving away from her toward the snack table. He walked over and grabbed a handful of pretzels, gazing at the pictures on the wall above the table. In each picture, Elizabeth's parents stood with celebrity after celebrity, smiling wide for the camera. Everyone from Tom Brady, to George Bush, to the Dali Lama was represented on the wall. Dontrell quickly noticed, however, that Elizabeth was absent from each and every picture. He suddenly began to feel guilty for treating her so poorly.

"Someone get this man a drink," someone whispered mockingly into his ear from behind. Turning around, Henry Galvin stood there in front of him, his perfectly faded, blonde hair parted off neatly to the side, and his round glasses covering his hazel eyes. Dontrell felt like he was back in the water, his pulse quickening with every second. "If I didn't know better, I'd say little Lizzy over there has a crush," Henry stated.

"She seems like a great girl," Dontrell replied with a smile, "but I don't think she's really my type."

"Remind me what your type is again," Henry questioned back.

Dontrell smiled, looking down on the floor. "How'd you get here?" he asked, hoping to change the subject before his friends noticed how flustered he felt.

"I walked," Henry stated. "Did you?"

"No," Dontrell responded, "I was studying at JJ's for a while beforehand, so I drove to his house and then drove him and the others here. I figured if it sucked, I'd have a way to escape."

"He seemed pissed at the race today," Henry stated. "Did everything go okay at home? I'm kind of surprised he let you out."

Embarrassed that Henry noticed, Dontrell looked down at the floor. "He doesn't know," Dontrell told him, then started to talk quieter. "He was out at a meeting, so it was just me and mom. I guess my lack of success drove him to want to drink, so he went to a meeting instead. I don't think he'd allow me out if he knew."

Without warning, Elizabeth's loud mouth joined the conversation. "I thought I told you that you deserved a drink? Can someone get the champion a drink?"

"It's really OK, Elizabeth, I'm…"

"We need a drink over here!" she continued unapologetically, clearly unaware of how to read the room around her. Most people were very relaxed, hanging out, socializing. There were about ten people total, so clearly not the wild party Elizabeth had hoped for, but that didn't seem to stop her from attempting to liven things up. Thinking of his mom, he knew she'd remind him that this was just Elizabeth's way of trying to feel loved, wanted. His heart went out for her, but he just wished she would go bother someone else.

"You know what?" Henry stepped in. "I'll go get him one. How about a Coke and rum?" He winked at Dontrell and headed toward the drinks. Elizabeth, satisfied with her success, walked away to seek attention from the group mesmerized by the television.

"Hen, you know—" Dontrell started.

"Of course," Henry interrupted, "I know. That's why you're going to take this cup of Coke." He handed him a cup and filled it with soda, "And our good friend Lizzy won't know the difference."

Dontrell was quickly reminded how grateful he was for his friend. Having kept his father's addiction a secret for so long, it finally felt nice to have someone who knew. It made it easier to talk about, to vent, but most importantly it made Dontrell feel like he could truly be himself. Growing up, it was always easier to keep it secret. There was a fear of judgment or gossip, plus his father had these strong beliefs about reputation and people's perception of the family. With Henry, it felt easy just to share it all. There were no secrets, and that made Henry the only person who truly understood him.

Feeling the urge to be alone, Dontrell asked, "Do you have a distractor? I need some air."

Henry pulled out a pack of cigarettes from his jacket pocket that he always kept there as a way to escape any situation he didn't want to be around. He walked around asking a few people, the ones who would notice if they went missing, if they needed a smoke break. They all declined—as he knew they would—so the two grabbed their jackets and headed out into the cold winter night. The snow had come down much faster over the last half-hour and was beginning to pile up on the ground. Trekking their way through the snow and away from the house, they made their way to a gazebo in the distance. Dontrell paused in his tracks, took a deep breath, and looked up toward the night sky. Something about the sound of snow falling relaxed him. It was almost like a natural white noise. For the first time all day, he felt truly happy.

"You know what this reminds me of?" he asked, spinning around in the snow. "Ebenezer Scrooge."

Henry smiled, remembering the time his class read *A Christmas Carol* in English the previous year. Never a fan of long, draw out stories, Dontrell struggled to find any redeeming qualities in the text. It was an old, long, and boring story about a selfish white man who regretted the choices he made. Nothing seemed overly exciting about that. It wasn't that he didn't like reading—put any Hunger Games book in front of him and it would be finished in mere hours, but the books he enjoyed were full of excitement, action. This story was definitely not.

It was four days before the final and Ms. Henninger, the English teacher, decided to partner students up in order to share their thoughts on the ending of the story.

"Dontrell Williams and Henry Galvin," she stated.

Disheartened he wasn't placed with one of his friends, Dontrell stood up and headed over to Henry's side of the room. "Hey," he stated, sticking his hand out to shake, "I'm Dontrell."

Henry shook his hand, "Henry. Nice to meet you."

Dontrell looked at him a little confused. "Are you new? I don't think I've seen you around much." It wasn't an overly large school, and after two years,

Dontrell was familiar with most faces. Dontrell also noticed that Henry had no idea who he was, which was rare at Fairview High.

"So what'd you think of the book?" Henry asked, jumping right in.

"It was great," Dontrell replied half-heartedly, looking up at the clock, anxiously awaiting the bell to ring.

Henry laughed, "Why don't you just admit you didn't read it?"

"Wow," Dontrell replied, "you're just going to assume I didn't read it?"

Henry smiled, "If you did, why don't you just tell me how you really felt about it?"

Dontrell picked up the book and held it in front of him. "This is the worst book I've ever read in my life. It's depressing, and slow, and more boring than watching paint dry."

Henry smiled. "Now that seemed much more honest."

"And you?" Dontrell asked. "I bet you loved it."

"That would be correct," Henry told him, "it's one of my favorites."

"You're joking," Dontrell stated, shocked at the fact that anyone could like such a book. "Have you read '*The Hunger Games*' or '*Harry Potter*' or any books written in the past decade? How can you like this?"

"I like the idea of redemption," Henry replied back justly. "This idea that no matter how badly we mess up in this world, there's always the chance to redeem ourselves."

Dontrell looked at him, surprised at the answer. It was the first intelligent response he'd heard about a book from anyone in this class. "What about a lack of redemption?" Dontrell asked.

"OK," Henry said, getting noticeably more excited. "Now we're having a discussion. What part of Scrooge's story shows a lack of redemption? He literally turns his life around."

"Yeah, that's easy to see if he's the only person you're looking at," Dontrell explains, "but what about Marley? No one ever stops to think that this story about redemption also shows the consequences of a lack of redemption. Where was Marley's chance to redeem himself?"

"It wasn't there," Henry replies.

"So who decides who gets redemption and who doesn't?" The second Dontrell's question ended, the bell rang and the students began their transition to the next class. Neither one of them moved; they both just stayed, staring at the other. "Well," Dontrell stated, grabbing his book and notebook, "it was really nice to meet you."

Henry stood up and stuck out his hand. "Yeah," he said, as Dontrell shook his hand back. "It was great to meet you too." The two stood there, shaking hands, looking into each other's eyes.

"Dontrell," some friends called out.

Letting go of Henry's hand, Dontrell turned to walk away.

"Oh god," Henry replied, now sitting down on the gazebo bench, staring at Dontrell laying in the snow. "Not Scrooge again. Haven't we spoken enough about him in Ms. Henninger's class?"

Dontrell ran over to the gazebo, "Yeah, but think about all he's given us! Without Scrooge, we never would have had coffee at Luna's Coffee Shop, which means I never would have told you about my swim meet and you never would have come to watch. Without Scrooge, we never would have had all those long drives around town or our special moment at Priker's Point. Without this grump of a man, we wouldn't be here together."

"Haha, are you sure you didn't sneak any rum into that Coke?" Henry laughed.

"I'm just happy," Dontrell replied, lying down next to him and resting his head in his lap. "I just love how calm the snow makes me feel. It's always so crazy to think about how right now, it's just snow. It isn't the annoying stuff that people have to shovel, or that causes accidents and power outages. Now, it literally is just beautiful frozen water falling from the sky. Something about it is just…calming."

Henry laughed.

"What?" Dontrell replied. "What is so funny about that?"

"That sounds like something your mom would say," Henry replied. "That's all."

"I'd rather hear that than the opposite," he replied. "I'd like to only be my mother and have no piece of my father in me at all."

"You don't mean that," Henry said.

"No!" Dontrell insisted, "I really do. I can't stand the man. I don't get why no matter how hard I try, no matter how patient I am, it's like we can never connect. Kemarion was his best friend. They did everything together. They even had jokes together, yet all I get is constant advice on how to be better, how to be stronger, how to be a better man. It's exhausting. I want to be nothing like him."

"Why do you think that is?" Henry questioned. "Why do you think he's constantly giving you advice?"

"Now you sound like my mom," Dontrell told him.

"I'm serious," Henry replied. "Why do you think that is?"

"Part of me thinks he misses Kemarion, so he feels the need to drink more, and one of his ways of coping is to focus on something else besides the alcohol. That ends up being me, my swimming, my grades, anything about my life that allows him to be intense, so he won't drink."

"What does the other part believe?"

Dontrell hesitated, "I'm afraid he might know."

Henry looked down at him, a level of understanding in his eyes that no one else would have. "You do?"

"My mom definitely does," he explained. "I'm sure of it. Today during dinner, she asked about you, and only you. I don't think she would have told him, but maybe deep down, he knows I'm hiding something. Maybe he senses there's a major difference between us, but doesn't know what it is, or maybe he's put the pieces together. I don't know."

"Sometimes, the fear of people finding out is greater than them actually knowing," Henry replied.

"Gee thanks, mom," Dontrell laughed.

"I'm serious," Henry urged nudging him gently. "I feared I'd lose all my friends, my family. I feared my life would fall apart. I worked myself sick worrying about what other people were going to say or do. Then I woke up one morning and realized I was the only one suffering. No one else around me felt sick to their stomach, just me. I was putting myself through more by not telling anyone than I would be if I just told them. So…I did and look at me now."

"I'm sure that wasn't easy. I'm sorry I never thought of that," Dontrell replied.

"You don't need to apologize," Henry assured. "I'm just saying…I get how hard it can be, but I also hate seeing you so worked up over what others will think while everyone else goes on with their lives."

"I'm afraid it'll drive him to drink," Dontrell admitted. "Like, what if this is the straw that breaks the camel's back? What if me telling him destroys our family? I can't do that to my mom. She's the one who got him to stop drinking, she's the one who got him to go to an AA meeting, she's the one who's been there supporting him from day one. I'm sure her life isn't going the way she hoped."

Henry placed his hand on Dontrell's face, softly rubbing his thumb along his cheek. "You're right. It could destroy your family, but it also might not. They might be fine but at the end of the day…will you? Will you be fine sneaking behind their backs your whole life? Will you be okay living a secret life just so they can continue to live theirs without knowing? Who does that remind you of?"

"My mother," Dontrell replied.

"Exactly. You just said her life hasn't gone the way she probably hoped, but now you're willing to do the same?"

Dontrell closed his eyes and took a deep breath. Henry was right. He watched his mother give up dream after dream in order to support his father's addiction and now here he was, living a lie just to support his father as well.

"I could become an alcoholic," he told Henry.

"What does that mean?" Henry asked.

"If I continue to live this way, it will continue to eat away at me. I'll continue to support my father while suffering at the same time. All of that will just get worse over time, and I can see myself needing a way to cope. It's why I don't drink. I can picture myself becoming him and lying about who I am will get me there the fastest."

"Well, you don't drink now," Henry reminded him. "So you've found another way to cope."

"Hmm, I did," Dontrell said with a smile as he grabbed Henry's face and pulled it closer to his. "I found you."

And the two shared a kiss in the quiet, snow-covered night.

Chapter 8
July 10th, 2012

Standing at the edge of St. Mary's park, I can feel the perspiration against my skin as Mason's grip on my hand tightens. Mason's eyes are focused straight ahead, as a handful of high school runners jog around the track surrounding the park, but I know his mind isn't with me right now.

"It'll be OK," I remind him, rubbing my thumb along his hand and guiding him across the track, dodging a few more afternoon runners, toward the crowd gathered on the lawn around the grills at the far end of the park.

He takes a deep breath, his confident, light-hearted stride now replaced with one of disappointment and embarrassment. "I don't know what to tell them if they ask," he says again, now hesitating outside the handball courts, while a bunch of older men cheer at the end of a point. "It was a god damn startup. I should have known better."

I turn to look at him, "You were right out of college. It was a great opportunity. You did nothing wrong. Everyone will understand that," I reassure him.

"I shouldn't have come," he tells me.

"Stop it," I remind him. "Everyone wants to see you. You've been avoiding them for weeks now. I can't keep making up lies about where you are."

A light breeze blows through the trees, making the hair sticking out of his backward Yankee hat move slightly. I watch Mason look around the park, past the handful of men and women moving past with their yoga mats rolled up beneath their arms, and his eyes find their way to the baseball diamond. He watches as a small child makes two failed attempts at hitting the ball. After giving him a minute, I place my hands on his face, pull it toward mine, and lock eyes with him.

"Look at me," I tell him when he attempts to turn away and avert eye contact. Finally, he stops resisting and looks at me, the shame hidden beneath those beautiful eyes. "It will be OK."

I smile at him one more time, grabbing his hand and pulling him in the direction of my family. His steps at first are labored, like a child forcefully being called back into the school after recess, but after a few seconds, he's back at my side as my father begins screaming out my name.

"Alex!" he yells across the picnickers enjoying their lunch, each of them looking up and over at me. A chorus of other noises, mostly inaudible shouts and cheers of joy from the family that surrounds him, accompany his yell. The volume in their voices doesn't change as we approach, but instead, it appears to get louder with each passing step. My cousin Eduardo is the first to greet us with a head nod and raised eyebrows, a solo cup being held in his mouth, while he juggles two massive plates of food.

We make our way over to my parents. My father, the king of the grill, puts down his spatula and throws his arms around me. "You made it!" he says to us, his accent barely noticeable after decades in the United States. "And you!" He grabs Mason by the shoulders and pulls him in for a hug. "You, my friend, have been away for too long!"

"So good to see you, Edgar," Mason replies. "I'm sorry it's been so long."

As he releases my father from the hug, my mother is standing there next in line. "Ah, I was so worried about you. I thought Alex might have scared you off!" she says to him, her accent oddly much thicker than my father's.

"Don't worry, Maria. She could never scare me off," Mason replies with a smile.

"How was the game?" she asks, pointing to our Yankee shirts. "Were your seats up close?"

Mason turns to look at me, unsure how to answer the question. "Well, we actually ended up not going," I explain to her. "Tickets were a little expensive, so we watched it right around the corner at a sports bar. The Yankees won though, so that's good!"

"You went all the way there and didn't even go inside?" my father asks in disbelief. "I can't remember the last time you went to a game. You should have just spent the money!" Out of the corner of my eye, I see Mason look toward the ground. My father makes the comment, unable to read the social cues around him, and then goes back to his cooking, grabbing the spatula and flipping a few burgers. My mother, however, doesn't miss a beat. By the time Mason looks back up at her with a fake smile on his face, she's already put the pieces together.

"How long has it been?" she asks softly, leading us farther away from my father.

Mason, again, looks to me. "About seven weeks," I tell her, sensing the shame emanating from Mason's eyes. "But we're very hopeful that something will come around soon."

"Seven weeks?" she asks. "Are you even able to pay your bills on one salary?"

"Everything will be fine, Mama," I reassure her. "Mason's been serving at Roberta's. We're good friends with the owner and he was gracious to give Mason a few shifts in the evening and on weekends, and I've taken on a few more hours at work to make a little extra overtime."

At the sound of the word "overtime," Mason lowers his head again. The truth is, I lied to him for the first couple of weeks, telling him I was taking a kickboxing class when instead, I agreed to temporarily take on some extra responsibilities at the office. While Mason was serving, I was at the office working. A few days ago, his shift got canceled and he was waiting for me when I got home four hours later.

"Well, do you need any help?" my mom asks. As she finishes the question, Mason's head pops back up.

"No, no, Maria," Mason explains. "That is so incredibly kind of you, but as Alex said, everything is going to be OK. I've had a few interviews already and have some more lined up. Really, we'll be fine."

I'll admit it was a good act. At least, it was good enough to convince my mom. She simply smiled, patted him on the shoulder, and went back to the picnic table to gossip about the neighbors with my aunts. I, however, know when Mason is full of bullshit.

"Are there more interviews lined up that we haven't discussed?" I ask him sarcastically while grabbing a plate and a heaping of rice.

"You know I've only had two interviews," he tells me in response. "I told you about them both."

I take a scoop of my grandmother's famous Chilaquiles before responding. "Oh, no. I knew about those. I was asking about the 'other' interviews you just told my mother about."

"C'mon, you know I just told her that to make her feel better," he informs me, putting some ketchup on his burger. "I don't want her to think we need her help."

Slamming my plate down on the table, I notice my cousins at the table closest to the food turn their heads. I quickly recognize the desire in their faces; they're praying for some drama. At some point, it always happens. Whether it's a sore loser after a soccer match, or a couple arguing in front of the food, there's always some form of drama.

Not from me though.

It will never be from me.

I smile and wave at them, letting Mason finish taking his last handful of chips before placing my hand on Mason's back and guiding him over toward the far table. He places his plate down and goes to take a bite of his burger.

"Are you serious right now?" I ask.

He looks at me confused; then, afraid he's missed something, he turns to look around at the others eating around us and engaged in conversation.

"You're going to start eating in the middle of this conversation?"

"Oh," he replies, placing the burger down on the plate, "I'm sorry. I thought we were done."

"No, we're not done. Of course, we aren't done," I whisper yell at him with a wide smile on my face to avoid any unwanted attention. "What makes you think we're done?"

He pauses for a second. "OK. I'm a little confused. Is your face OK? It almost looks like you're having a seizure."

I stare at him in utter disbelief. The brain in his head holds so much valuable information, and it's gotten him so far in life, but there are these moments when it's like he's turned it off completely. While I'm looking directly at him, I can see his eyes repeatedly moving from mine, back down to the burger.

"You know what," I say to him. "You eat. I'll be over there when you're finished." Grabbing my plate, I get up from the table and talk toward the bench at the edge of the park. The second I sit down, Mason's already next to me, plate in his hand.

"What is the matter?" he asks me, this time his eyes only on mine. "I've watched you lie to your mother before, so I know you aren't upset about that."

I hesitate, trying to find the right words. "We don't need her money, but I also don't understand why you are so afraid to ask for help."

"I just don't want your parents to have to worry, that's all," he tells me, giving me another bullshit answer.

"That's a lie and we both know it," I inform him. "It's more than just the money, Mason. I didn't find out you lost your job until two days later. Why?"

I watch him stare off at the cars in the distance as he thinks about his response. "I'm not good with asking for help," he finally admits. "I didn't tell you about the job because I was embarrassed. I should have seen the warning signs. I literally worked for a failing company for years and somehow missed it. Then I'm told I'm not only losing my job but that the company has no money, no severance, nothing. I felt like an idiot, and I didn't want you to see me fail. I was hoping I'd have another job lined up and ready to go, and then I'd tell you. I never imagined I'd have to wait this long."

I place my hand on his back, right between his shoulders, and begin to rub up and down. "Mason, I'm your partner, and I love you more than anything. You can't be afraid to ask me for help. You don't have to do these things alone anymore."

Suddenly, I feel the bench lightly vibrate, and Mason reaches down for his phone. He looks at the number and then looks back to me. His eyes widen in disbelief as he answers the phone.

"Hello?

"Yes, this is Mason.

"Hi, sir. How are you?

"Well, I'm great. Thanks for asking.

"Yes, sir.

"Yes, sir.

"Yes, sir.

"Excellent, sir. I look forward to speaking with you more.

"You too, sir."

He hangs up the phone and turns to look at me. A genuine smile crosses his face for the first time in weeks.

"So, that was Lincoln Memorial Hospital," he tells me. "They want to offer me the job."

"Mason!" My smile is now as big as his. "That's amazing! Isn't that the PR Coordinator position?"

"Well, it was," he tells me, "but they don't want me to do that."

I pause, waiting for him to finish, but the end of that sentence never comes out. Instead, he just sits there in disbelief, a woman with a stroller walking by, staring back down at the ground.

"What position is it then?" I ask him.

"They want me to be the Director of Marketing and Communications, like they want me to be in charge of the entire department. Apparently, their Director recently left and they wanted to bring in a fresh perspective. He raved about my previous work, and told me I was exactly what he was looking for."

Staring at him in amazement, I can't help but feel an overwhelming feeling of being so proud. I hug him tightly, grateful that he's here with me. Like a seven-week curse that is finally lifted, I can see him sit up a little tighter, and I can see the light begin to reappear in his eyes.

"Mason," I say to him. He turns to look at me with a grin. "It is okay to ask for help, especially from me. It will never make you appear weak. It will never make you a failure. Do you understand me?"

He's looking at me and nodding with each word I speak, yet I know he isn't truly listening to me. Deep down, I know it's his biggest weakness; this inability to admit he needs help. Not wanting to ruin the happy moment, I know I need to let it go, so I simply rub his hand one more time and remind him, "I'm so proud of you."

"Now," he says to me, standing up and taking my hand and looking back toward my family. "Why don't we go and have a good time?"

Chapter 9
September 7th, 2014

The world is asleep, yet I am awake. Looking around the park, listening to the silence, I can't help but think about what silence truly means. If silence is, in fact, silence then why do I feel like it's something I can hear. It's like a sound, but it can't be because it's silence. It is this exact thought that has me out of bed as the sun rises on a beautiful Saturday morning. A Saturday morning, I might add, that should find me sleeping soundly in my bed, next to the love of my life.

It *should* find me there.

I, however, am found here, sitting alone on a wooden park bench, listening to the silence around me. If I sit here long enough, maybe, just maybe I'll become part of the silence. I'll become part of the silence long enough to understand what it means, what it represents.

This isn't the first time I've come to this park and sat on this bench at this hour of the morning. In fact, I consider this my bench. No, it doesn't actually belong to me, but I like to think it feels a stronger connection to me than to the other bench-sitters it serves. It is these people, these park-goers, these bench sitters that bring me here many Saturday mornings.

Imagine a world where people, people from all walks of life, are all connected. It isn't a connection, like favorite sports team, or food, but a deeper, more profound connection.

A bench.

I am sitting on this bench, the same bench I've sat on multiple times in my life. I'm listening to the silence, allowing it to guide my thoughts, my feelings. This bench helps me connect to those I do not know, to those I do not understand.

Who sat here before me?

Who is going to sit here after?

Why are they here?

The single mom, who's watching her son play on the jungle gym, sits here worrying about the overwhelming burden her finances cause and her desire to provide her son with a life of joy. The immigrant sits here, proud of the hard work he put in to build a life in this country, but guilt for leaving family behind. Former lovers sit here, discussing how to explain their divorce to their children. Current lovers sit here, planning, and look toward their future.

It's a simple bench, yet its story is a masterpiece, a heartbreak, a glimmer of hope.

So I sit here, listening to the silence, feeling everyone's love, pride, and heartbreak. I feel their anxiety, their guilt, but also feel a connection. It's a connection to others I may never meet, but I feel and understand their stories.

Connection.

I also leave behind my own story.

Growing up in the Bronx, I felt like there was connection everywhere. No one had to be family. You were all connected under a culture, a belonging, and I never knew anyone felt anything different, so I made the assumption that life was like that everywhere.

I was wrong.

I quickly realized after I left for school that connection wasn't something that came easily. Sure, friends are there to support you, to help you get through tough times, to laugh with you, but do they understand you? Not the person you show on the outside, but the person embedded in your core. I found it easy to show most people the external person, but none saw the internal.

There was just a lack of connection.

That lack of connection led me to this bench every day for years. It helped me understand that I was more connected to others than I ever thought I could be.

Then, he came along.

I look up, as the leaves shuffle in the distance, and I see he's standing against a tree, just watching me. There's this smile on his face—it's the same smile he has every time he catches me here.

It's a smile that connects.

As he walks toward me, sweat pants and a t-shirt somehow making him look like a God, I can't help but think about all the times we've connected on this bench.

He hands me a coffee. "Good morning," his words melting my heart, and making me weak in the knees. Almost four years and his words still have the same effect they did when we first met.

"A very good morning," I reply back to him, giving him a kiss.

"Would you like some company?" he asks, always checking if I'm ready.

I slide over, making room for him to sit.

"I always want your company," I remind him, taking another sip of coffee and letting the heat spread throughout my body.

We continue to sit in silence. I see him, out of the corner of my eye, put his head back, take a deep breath, and close his eyes. He's trying to understand, trying to feel what I feel each time I come here. Deep down, I know he never will understand. It isn't something many people ever would understand, but the fact that he's trying, that just proves how much he loves me. It only solidifies the connection that I feel to him on a daily basis.

The connection to someone who can see my soul.

I don't know how it happened, or even when it happened. It isn't something I can really pinpoint. There is no moment in time when suddenly I could feel him connected to me, but there are moments, small moments, when I could sense the connection getting deeper.

I grab his hand. Opening his eyes, startled, he takes a deep breath and clears his throat.

"You were sleeping," I laugh at him, "weren't you?"

"Absolutely not!" he declares defensively. "I was soaking in all the emotions."

"You are such a liar!" I accuse him, poking him in the stomach to get the truth out of him.

Squirming, he begins to laugh.

"Fine! Fine," he shouts out, desperately trying to protect his stomach from my pokes. "It's just so early, Al. I couldn't help it."

"You could sleep in your own bed," I remind him. "I left a note, you knew where I was"

"Exactly. I knew where you were, so I had to come," he tells me, with a mischievous smile on his face. As he starts kissing my neck, I push him away.

"You really thought you'd come out here to get lucky?" I ask him, shocked at his thinking.

"Well," he says to me, in that sweet angelic voice he uses to get his way, "I'm already lucky."

A smile creeps across his face, as he stares to get my reaction. I smile back and lean against his shoulder as he puts his arm around me.

"...but I mean, I could be luckier," he says lightly.

Pushing him away again, I slide to the far end of the bench. "I can't believe you thought I would sleep with you out here," I say to him.

He looks at me, confused.

"Again," he states.

"What?" I ask.

"You meant to say, how you weren't going to sleep with me out here again," he tells me.

"I don't know what you mean," I say, looking around to make sure no one else is in the park.

He starts to laugh and stands up from the bench. He starts to walk away before turning around and throwing his arms out to the side like he's addressing an audience. "LADIES AND GENTLEMEN OF THE PARK," he screams out. Mortified, I look around again to see if anyone heard him. It's mostly empty with the exception of an early-riser getting in a morning walk.

"Mase," I beg him, "it is six in the morning."

He ignores my pleas.

"I HAVE MADE LOVE TO THIS WOMAN ON THIS BENCH."

"Mase, stop it," I hush to him.

"AND…IT WAS HER IDEA!"

I run to him, throwing my hand over his mouth. Picking me up, he carries me back to the bench and sits down.

"I hate you," I tell him, as I slowly remove my hand from his mouth, ready to cover it back up if he starts to make any more declarations.

"I'm sorry," he whispers to me with a smile, "but everyone deserved to know the truth."

"Having sex in public is a misdemeanor. It isn't something to announce to the world," I inform him.

"So you're admitting it happened?" he asks.

"I'm saying it's illegal and shouldn't be spoken about," I tell him.

"I'm sorry. I will talk to the animals on our way out and make sure they don't say anything," he jokes with me. "I won't ever deny that it happened though. It was the best night of my life."

As embarrassing as it may be, the night was…one to remember.

"I just keep thinking about those unfortunate people who had to sit on the bench the next day," I confess.

"I'm sure they had no idea," he tells me.

"That's not the point," I quickly remind him. "This bench is the connection between so many random people who have never met. The stories this bench holds are so diverse and meaningful. I can't help but think we ruined that."

He points to a carving on the bench.

"I'm going to assume 'Jeremy <3 Rachel' ruined it first," he tells me.

"I don't know if that makes me feel better or worse. The fact that others had the same idea we did."

"Close your eyes," he tells me. I'm hesitant after his last stunt, but decide to give him a chance. "Picture a couple walking around the park. They're in their mid-30s and they've been struggling to find that connection they had when they first got married. Their relationship had begun to unravel years before with life getting so busy that they simply forgot to take the time out for each other. It's their first date night since having their third child. It started with a movie, a place where you can easily avoid talking, and when it ended, they began to walk home. It was on this walk that both realized they hadn't had a meaningful conversation in years. They look at each other, wondering where it all started to fall apart. The snow begins to fall gently around them as they enter the park. Both are afraid to go home, afraid to go back to the reality that is their struggling marriage, so they sit down on this park bench. They don't talk. They just sit in silence watching the snowfall around them, accumulating on the grass, the swings, and the trees.

"After a few minutes, Jeremy takes his keys out of his pocket and begins to rub them along the bench. Rachel, annoyed at the broken silence, asks him to stop. When she turns though, to look at the damage he's done to the bench, she sees he's written 'Jeremy <3 Rachel.' Her heart begins to beat faster as she looks up and for the first time in years, and sees the man she fell in love with all those years ago."

He ends his story there.

"Where did you read that?" I ask him.

"Nowhere," he tells me. "I just made it up. For all we know, that marking on this bench saved their marriage. The markings on this bench might have changed the course of someone's life."

All this time, I believed that I was the only one who truly understood the connection to the people who have used this bench. Clearly, I was wrong.

"Do you remember what else happened on this bench?" he asks me, as he puts his arm around me again, letting me rest my head on his shoulder.

Of course, I remembered. This bench was more than just a place to enjoy the silence. Every important moment in our relationship happened on this bench.

"We had just finished coming back from dinner," I start to tell him. "You were wearing your tight, muscle-hugging, button-up shirt—you know, the one with the thin blue lines making that checkered pattern. And your jeans, oh my, those skinny jeans that made your butt look way too good."

I take a sip of coffee, but thinking about that day, there is a warmth already running through my body. "You had made this joke, this really bad joke, about Batman and church. Like, what do you call Batman who skips out on church?"

"Oh yeah," he smiles while laughing, "Christian Bale. Best joke I have."

"Well, I remember how offended you got when I didn't laugh. Then you tried to explain it to me like I wasn't smart enough to understand it."

"Christian," he says to me dumbfounded, "like people who go to church are Christians. Then his last name is Bale, like to bail from something, but just spelled differently."

"Yeah, you said something like that," I laugh back at him. "Then you got even more flustered when I paid for ice cream while your back was turned."

"I turned around for two seconds and you had already paid. I don't understand how you did it that fast?" he reminds me.

"Anyway," I move on, unwilling to listen, "we walked into the park and sat down here to eat. You started talking about the stars, about how crazy it was that there were other people just like us, sitting on a bench just like this, all out there in the distance. Watching you speak, seeing the amazement in your eyes, just made me realize how different you were from anyone else I'd ever dated."

"Somewhere out there is an alternate universe, I'm telling you," he reminds me.

"I know, Mase, I know," I reassure him.

"You told me about this bench," he says.

"I did. I told you about this bench," I admit.

"If you told me about this bench on the first date, I might have thought you were crazy and ran away," he jokes.

"No, you wouldn't have," I tell him. "There was something there, in your eyes, and in your voice. The way you spoke to me, the way you looked at me, I knew I could tell you anything and you wouldn't run."

"I did the opposite of run," he replies.

"You kissed me and told me you loved me," I tell him. "You listened to me speak, you waited until I was done, and you kissed me."

"I realized I was in love," he tells me. "I realized every single person that came before you was only there to lead me to you."

The light from the sun spreads throughout the park as the morning begins to break. The park isn't as quiet as before, now that the hustle and bustle of the day has begun. Early morning runners, parents pushing strollers with wide-awake babies, and even the birds have all graced us with their presence. Everything starts to happen around us, but all I can focus on is Mason.

"I have always struggled to find the words to truly tell you how I feel," he tells me. A serious look crosses his face, and his nerves are evident in the shakiness of his voice. "It's funny because you've been the person who has helped me talk about my feelings, but they've always been emotions about other people, or other events. You got me to talk about my father the first day we met, and you got me to express myself in ways I never imagined. You have not, however, helped me figure out how to tell you how I feel."

He swallows and takes a deep breath. I don't know why, but I feel a giant pit in my stomach. "I have tried, many times, to show you, to treat you in a way that helps you understand how I feel. You've accepted me for who I am, your family has taken me in as their own, even though I'm not from the Bronx."

I laugh.

"And you're white," I remind him. He laughs and loosens up for the first time since speaking.

"And white," he repeats. "It didn't matter to you or them who I was in my past, or where I came from. You only cared about who I am right now and who I want to be in the future."

He starts to stand up and places his hand inside his jacket pocket. "I told you on our first date I believed I had a purpose in life. Do you remember what I said?"

"You told me that you thought I was your purpose. You said your purpose was to spend as much time with me as you possibly could."

He pulls out a box, as he gets down on one knee. The pit in my stomach has exploded into a swarm of butterflies. Yes, butterflies because a moment like this feels too light and happy.

"I know who I am. It is clearer than it ever has been. I also know who I want to be in the future." He opens the box and the sun reflects off the diamond, perfectly shaped, sitting on top of a white gold band.

"I want to be your husband," he tells me as he takes his finger and points to a spot on the bench right below the far-left corner. I look closely at the engraving and it reads:

"Will you marry me?"

I'm instantly brought back to his words: The markings on this bench might have changed the course of someone's life. His markings, this bench, are changing the course of our lives together. I never pictured the ring, but I've always pictured this moment, the moment when the love of my life asks me if I want to spend the rest of my life with him. I've always pictured it being magical, radiant, life-changing.

This moment is nothing like I ever imagined.

It's even better.

It's even better because of the man kneeling before me. The man I know was meant for me.

"I would love to," I tell him, tears streaming across my face. He leans in to kiss me and wraps his strong arms around me. It's those arms that will always be wrapped around me, keeping me warm when it's cold, cheering me up when I'm unhappy, sharing the excitement with me when I'm glad. It is that face that I get to wake up to every morning.

That is my man.
That is my future husband.
And I cannot wait.

Chapter 10
Session 3

Staring up at the unpleasant, vine-covered carriage house, I can't help but feel a pit in my stomach. Walking the path toward the house was excruciatingly difficult, my feet like brakes attempting to stop me in my tracks. The red door stares back at me, reminding me how my spirit was dismantled behind that door one week ago. Once again, everything in my body tells me to turn around, to run, but the paper in my hand tells me this is where I need to be.

As I get to the stoop, I realize I'm five minutes early, so I step off to the side and take the pack of American Spirits out of my back pocket. Almost on cue, like she'd been spying on me from inside the home, McKnight opens the door. She still sports the same, bright, cheery smile she showed last week. The difference is that this time I know it's all an act. The woman's a warrior, out for blood. The smile is just a front to get others to let their guard down. She's wearing a brighter top, similar to last time, but today she has on jeans. It's a much more comfortable look, which sends the impression she's ready for anything I throw her way.

"Mason, welcome," she states again in that same pleasant voice like she's genuinely happy to see me. "I love your punctuality; please, come on in."

Using my own punctuality against me, like showing up five minutes early means I'm happy to be here. I quickly shove my cigarette and lighter back into my front pocket, as she watches me like a hawk, and head up the stoop and into the room. Entering the room, once again, feels comforting as the birch wood smell starts to calm my beating heart. Looking around the room, everything is exactly as I remember, except for the owls. Each owl has been transitioned around the room to a new location. As I sit down on the couch, I notice that the owl sitting on the table next to me is no longer calm, with its wings beginning to open up. Now, the owl next to me has its wings spread wide, and is holding onto the branch with only its toes like it's about to push off and fly away.

"It's different," I state, the first words I've spoken to her today, but I continue to stare at the owl as I say them.

"Yes. They all are," she reassures me. "I move them every week to different spots."

"What's the point?" I question her, not hiding the fact that I think it sounds like a lot of unnecessary work.

"Like us," she calmly explains, "the owls are on a journey too."

"These wooden owls," I ask boldly, as I pick up the owl next to me and shake it in front of her face. "They are on a journey?"

Anger crosses her face for the first time, as she eyes my hand squeezing the owl. It's the first negative emotion I've seen cross her face since we met. Instantly realizing I've made a terrible mistake, I gently place the owl back down on the table and rest my hands into my pockets. "I'm very sorry," I reassure her. "I shouldn't have touched your belongings."

She stares at me as silence hits the air, and I awkwardly stand in the middle of the room. At this moment, I get the feeling she is either thinking of what to say next or plotting to kill me. Either way, I'm terrified of what's to come.

"Please...sit down," she says to me, gesturing for me to sit. A smile crosses her face, like one of those smiles you'd see from a person who's about to rip out your soul. "Do you remember your first week," she begins, the anger gone from her eyes, but replaced with a more intense determination, "when you mentioned you felt confused?"

"Yes. Yes, I do," I tell her. Resisting her questions doesn't seem like the right choice at the moment, so I work on easing the tension in the room.

"I feel a very similar way right now," she informs me, and then just sits there and stares. She doesn't look at the owl, doesn't look out the window— she just stares directly into my eyes reminding me that fear of eye contact is not a weakness for her.

I lean back against the couch for support, as the weight of her stare sinks into my core. Unsure if I should speak, or continue basking in the silence, I simply stare back. Seconds feel like minutes, as they slowly tick along.

I can no longer take the silence.

"Why are you confused?" I finally ask her, my words like a knife cutting through the silence. Yet, she doesn't respond right away. She continues to sit there, staring. Like a book, wide open, I can feel her reading my every thought, every move. When she blinks, she pauses with her eyes closed, takes a deep breath in, opens her eyes and crosses her legs.

"I find myself confused," she finally speaks after what feels like hours, "because I believe we share these genuine moments; moments of openness, kindness, honesty. Then, it's like you catch yourself being you, and decide that

that isn't OK, so you become this heated, angry, frustrated person. I believe you walk in here and think that if you put up a front, it will hide the suffering and pain you feel inside. Last week, for example, we ended on really good terms. We were being open and honest with each other and I felt you trusted my intent. Today, however, you come in here angry. I'm going to assume that you use this anger because it's worked before. Someone, at some point in your life, stopped digging because you acted fine. This person, whoever it was, taught you that if you continue to act and put up this front, that no one will ever catch the pain that lies beneath the surface."

Shit.

"Would you say this is a fair assumption?" she asks me.

My brain isn't spinning, my panic alarms aren't going off, and I don't feel like I'm being ambushed. For the first time, looking at her, I sense the authenticity of her thoughts and feelings. She no longer seems like the enemy, prepared to attack at any sign of weakness, but now she presents herself as an ally, prepared to help fight off any unwarranted attack. In fact, she reminds me of Alex, unafraid to push through the armor to see what's underneath.

"It is," I respond to her softly, clearing my throat.

"…and this person, the person who never dug any deeper, who would that be?" she asks, trying to dig deeper herself.

"My mother," I confess, unafraid of the truth. This truth isn't important any longer, so I have no fear of speaking about it.

"Why do you think she never dug deeper? Why do you think she always assumed everything was OK?"

"…because I made her believe it all was," I confess.

"What do you mean by that?" she asks as she leans forward in her chair, resting her elbows on her knees. It's the first time since I've met her that I've seen her lean so far forward, seen her close the distance between us, which makes this question seem very important to her.

"It was my job to make everyone believe that things were going to turn out all right," I admit to her, as I feel my body loosen up, the tension from holding back the truth slowly starting to fade away.

"Why was it your job and not someone else's?" she asks in return.

"Well, my brother and sister were way too young, so they barely understood what was happening around us, let alone how to handle it all," I explain to her, as I stare at the owl sitting next to me.

"If you don't mind me asking, what about your parents? Why couldn't they handle a job like this?" As she asks the question, she places her pen and notebook down on the table next to her. It's the first time it hasn't been in her hands since we met.

I begin to question whether or not I want to answer the question, whether or not I'm comfortable sharing this information. To this day, one person has heard this story and no one else. It is the chink in my armor, my Achilles heel, and when you share your weakness with others, it begins to feel demoralizing. It consumes you and begins to haunt your every waking day. It's a crutch that you now have to limp around with all day, hoping that no one comes to kick it out from under you.

"If you are uncomfortable with the question, we can leave it unanswered for now," she tells me, giving me an escape route for the first time. "I can imagine answering this question might feel like you're losing control."

Torn with the need to be honest, but the desire to maintain control, I hesitate to respond. McKnight allows the silence to return, unafraid to sit in it for moments at a time. She watches, as I move my eyes across the bookshelves, to the owls standing proud and tall on top of the fireplace, and finally to the door.

"You're thinking about leaving," she says to me. It isn't a question; she isn't asking me if I'm thinking about leaving, she's telling me that I am thinking about leaving. And she's right. I'd be lying if I said walking out didn't cross my mind—it was the only thing that crossed my mind as I stared at the red door.

Bringing my gaze back to her, I remain silent, unsure where this conversation goes next. I'm the weakest person in the room for the first time in a long time, yet a large part of me doesn't care.

"Why are you thinking about leaving?" she asks, knowing that her statement was correct.

"Leaving is easier than this," I inform her. "Leaving allows this conversation to end."

She sits there and nods. "Leaving lets you maintain control," she reminds me.

"It helps me maintain control," I confirm.

"You're right," she says, plain and simple.

Confused by the statement, I look at her, waiting for her to continue. Only, she doesn't continue, she just looks at me. She motions toward the door, encouraging me to go. I, however, just sit there.

Grabbing the piece of paper I gave her when I walked in off the table, she signs it and hands it to me.

"You have what you need. The paper is signed. If you want to leave, then leave." Her tone isn't mad, or disappointed, it's completely positive. I could stand up and walk out of this office right now, and she wouldn't come after me.

"Look," she says to me, "I'll even sign the other spots. You never have to come back. Just give this to your parole officer and call it a day."

I sit still; not frozen, not stuck, just still, unsure what choice to make.

"You haven't left yet," she informs me, almost as if I don't know.

"I know," I reply back, with a tone of frustration in my voice.

"Why not?" she pushes more, almost mad this time like she's angry I haven't walked out of her office and left her alone. "Why have you not left?" she repeats herself, the tone unwavering.

"I don't know!" I yell back. "I don't know!"

"What do you mean, you don't know?" She's yelling now, too. "If you want to leave, then LEAVE!"

My anger and frustration builds. I thought our previous week's session was tense, but this—this has suddenly reached a whole new level. I rest my head in my hand, not even trying to hide my frustration.

She leans forward in her chair so her face is right in front of mine, and she repeats her demanding question one more time, quieter but with the same force as before. "Why have you not left?" Each word emphasized by an intense amount of weight in her tone.

"I DON'T WANT TO LEAVE!" I finally scream back, shaking my hands close to her face. My face reflects a dark shade of red. As I finish screaming the sentence, she simply leans back into her chair, crosses her leg, and smiles.

She knew I wouldn't leave.

Now, much more gently, much calmer, she tells me, "I didn't leave either."

I look at her, confused.

"When my husband's drinking became a problem, when my family struggled to keep it together—I never left. I stayed and I fought. It's the same reason you won't walk out that door right now. You are a fighter. You do not quit, and you will get through this. Do you believe me when I say that?"

"I don't know," I admit to her.

"Well," she continues, "do you at least trust that I'm going to do my best to help you get through it?"

I pause and look up at her, staring into her hazel eyes. "I think I do."

"Good," she replies. "Let's start by telling me who forced you to take on the problems of the world, without ever focusing on your own?"

My hands shaking, I take multiple, large deep breaths in and out. Her question lingers in the air, waiting for me to calm myself down. My fists are clenched. My heart is racing. I close my eyes, inhale, look up to the ceiling, and exhale. I sit like that, with my head still facing the ceiling, for a few seconds, before I finally bring it back down and place my eyes on her.

"My father," I inform her.

She nods and continues to stare. This time, she waits, as she lets me find the words to continue the story.

"When my father left, it was," I hesitate, forcing myself to relive the memories, "tough for my family. My mother fell apart. She stopped taking care of herself and stopped taking care of my brother and sister. I was old enough to understand that the depression was slowly destroying her, getting worse with each and every passing day. My brother and sister struggled to understand why our father left and why our mother stopped caring. Someone needed to step up, to take responsibility, so that burden fell to me."

I stop and look down at my hands.

"They needed someone to help them see that everything was going to be all right," I tell her. "I did everything I could to make sure their lives were as normal as possible. Over time, the more I convinced her everything would be OK, the better my mom became."

"Did your mother speak to anyone, about what happened, or about her depression?" McKnight asks me, her voice filled with sorrow.

"Twice a week, every week. I think she still sees someone," I tell her.

"And what about your brother and sister? Did they speak to anyone about it all?"

"At the time, money was pretty tight," I explain to her. "My mom took a leave of absence from work, so we lost our health insurance. I was going to school during the day, and working two jobs in the evening, but there wasn't any money to pay for therapy. I did, however, make sure they had a standing appointment with their school counselor each week. It was the best I could do."

"Did that seem to work?" she asks.

"It did. Most kids have chores around the house; my brother and sister had counseling. If they didn't go, they'd lose TV time or be grounded for the weekend."

She smiles, amused by that part of the story.

"And you'd enforce those rules," she asks as a follow-up.

I smile, "Oh, you bet I did. I wasn't exactly the most liked brother at the time, but it was what they needed and they'll admit that to you now."

"That smile," she states, pointing to the one on my face, "it's the first time I've seen you genuinely happy since I met you. You seem…proud."

"Damn right I was proud," I inform her. "I held that family together, and at the age of 16 too."

"That must have been hard, though, to be so young and have so much responsibility?" she asks.

"It held me back a little," I admit. "I had a choice to let my family fall apart, let my grades fall apart, or let my social life fall apart."

"Judging by your Ivy League education, I'm going to assume the social life got the cut," she infers.

"It did," I tell her.

"That doesn't surprise me—that you were able to be that strong," she tells me, with a smile across her face. "I am curious, though." She pauses, clearly for dramatic effect. "…did you ever talk to someone about everything that happened?"

I nod my head to indicate no.

"How did you work through everything that happened? All that stress, responsibility, all of those feelings."

I sit there, staring out the window, watching the light from the sun beginning to fade as it set in the evening sky, wondering how I did work through all those feelings. Thankfully, I don't need to respond. It's her turn to do the talking.

"I'm willing to bet that you didn't work through it," she states.

I let a gentle laugh out, nod my head, and embarrassingly shrug my shoulders. "I started smoking," I tell her. "It was the only thing that relieved the stress."

"Smoking can be an expensive habit," she tells me, like I haven't already figured that out.

"It was," I admit, "but it was something that calmed me down in less than five minutes. It was immediate, much faster and cheaper than a 45-minute counseling session…no offense."

She laughs, "None taken."

"Smoking helped me relax. It made me feel like my problems were disappearing," I tell her.

"What about your swimming?" she asks. "I'm sure the smoking didn't help you get better."

"I actually didn't smoke when I swam in college," I admit. "When I started on the team my freshman year, I found it had the same effect as cigarettes. It wasn't until after college, when the swimming stopped, that I fell back into the habit."

"You've heard of Pandora's box, right?" she asks, as she grabs her water bottle, takes a sip, and places it back down on the table.

After these three sessions, I'm not surprised by her left-field comment. In fact, I'm surprised it took her this long to make one.

"Of course. Pandora finds a box, filled with the evils of the world, and opens it, unleashing it all onto the people," I reply back.

"See, most people believe that Pandora is the problem in the story," she begins and suddenly, I see her finding another gray area in a clearly right versus wrong type of story.

"How can you not blame her?" I ask in shock. "She opened a box she was told not to open."

"Well, of course, Pandora is partially to blame," she admits. "She was told not to open the box, and she did. Zeus, however, everyone's favorite hero, is never blamed for giving the box to Pandora."

I know there's going to be a point to this story, but I'm struggling to figure out what it could possibly be. Suddenly, I feel like I'm back at Princeton, listening to my professor's words and struggling to comprehend where they are heading. Oddly enough, I find myself anxious and excited, waiting for her to work her magic, and pull some abstract lesson from thin air.

"Where was her explanation? Why did Zeus trust her with the box, but not with the knowledge about what was inside? Do you think if Pandora knew what was inside the box, that she would have opened it?"

I'm so caught up in her passion for the story, that I don't even realize she's waiting for me to respond. "Oh," I reply, completely off guard, "no. I guess I don't think she would have opened it."

"Exactly!" she exclaims, pleased at my chosen answer. She waits, letting me ponder everything she's just explained. A week ago, I would have continued to stare at her, waiting for her to speak, or I would have asked her what the point was to her stupid story. Today, however, I somehow understand.

"I never told anyone what was inside Pandora's box," I reply.

She smiles, clearly pleased at my response. Then she crosses her legs, folds her arms, and gives me the hand signal to continue.

"I am Pandora's box. I hold, tightly, onto my emotions. I push the bad ones deeper and deeper; until I convince myself they are no longer there. They never disappear, though. They stay there, festering, building, waiting for the box to be opened."

For the first time, in a long time, I feel truly powerful.

"Hiding your emotions hasn't made you more powerful," she informs me. "In fact, they make your own weaknesses invisible."

"I had no idea what was going to happen at the grocery store," I admit to her, willingly talking about it for the first time since it happened.

"Every truly powerful person in this world," she tells me, "isn't blind to his or her weaknesses. They know more about their weaknesses than anybody else and *that* is what makes them strong. Knowing what causes your weaknesses, allows you to fix them, to adjust to them, and to learn to handle them."

I just stare, amazed that a week ago, this woman was the bane of my existence, and now, I find myself drawn to her.

"Let's start with your first blaring weakness," she informs me.

I look at her, surprised that she'll simply tell me my weakness.

"We need to talk about your father," she tells me matter-of-factly. "Right now."

"OK," I tell her, confident for the first time that this can make me the man I want to become, "I'm ready."

"How do you feel about your father leaving?" she asks me.

I think for a minute, unsure of what emotion, what word to use for such an experience. Walking out on your 16-year-old son and never reaching out leaves a lot of unopened wounds. "First," I begin, "I feel anger."

"Good," she replies back, satisfied with my response. "Why anger?"

I take a deep breath—just thinking about it makes my face flush with frustration.

"Who the hell does that?" I pause, to unclench my fists and try to relax.

"It's OK," she informs me, "let your anger show."

"Sixteen god damn years. He was my father for 16 years and suddenly he decides one day he wants to stop. Did it become too hard? He was an adult! He had responsibilities." I stop, again, take a deep breath, and try to continue with my voice much calmer. "I just don't understand," I explain to her. "No, my childhood wasn't perfect. We weren't the ideal family. I know that, but we were his kids. We were *his*. How do you walk out on someone who is part of you?"

Silence envelops the room again. I just can't continue to find the right words. I want to, I truly do, but I find myself searching for help.

"When you say your childhood wasn't perfect, what do you mean?" She asks me, aware that I was in need of a little push.

"The man was an ass. There isn't a doubt in my mind that he had an anger problem. I don't have a memory of him smiling or laughing. He was a very angry man all the time."

"Angry?" she asks.

"Abusive, well, at least emotionally. He never had to be physically abusive. Everyone was scared shitless of him. Throwing things, smashing things, punching holes through walls, he never hit a single one of us, but that doesn't mean it didn't feel like abuse. No one left the house with visible marks or scratches, but we left the house with fear."

"That must have been hard," she interjects.

I stop to think about that statement because, in reality, it never felt hard for me. Yes, I felt that fear, I lived in that fear, but that was my life. I grew accustomed to it, adapted to it. "I think it was the worst on my mom," I tell her. "It slowly destroyed her, one day at a time. When he left, I really thought things would get better."

"But they didn't," she states.

"No, they didn't. Well, I guess it depends on what you consider better. No one was in fear anymore, no one walked around on eggshells, afraid to upset him. A new fear, though, slowly emerged once he left."

She looks at me, curious.

"We feared we weren't going to make it," I tell her. "We feared the bills wouldn't be paid, feared the heat would go off, food wouldn't make it on the table. We feared we'd lose everything."

"...and your mother shut down," she states.

"Within days," I inform her. "The day he left; she didn't get out of bed. That one day turned into two, and five, and ten, and then I realized she wasn't coming out of that room. At least, the mother I knew wasn't coming out of that room. So, I went out, got a job. I started working at the local bike shop after school, fixing and selling bikes. Then when the shop closed for the evening, I'd leave the shop and head to the local diner where I was the busboy until ten or 11 each night and even later on the weekends. It was a lot, yeah, but I brought in some money. I paid for the food. I paid the bills. I'd ask around different doctors' offices, riding around town on my bike, if they knew of an affordable therapist. I even found one who was willing to come to the house."

"You were a resourceful man...and a brave one," she tells me. "Many people would have crumbled under that pressure."

I laugh a little and nod my head.

"You know, you are the first person to say that to me," I inform her. "It sounds so goddamn ungrateful, but I never even got a thank you. I am the reason that woman is alive right now and she acts like it never happened."

"Why do you think she hasn't said that?" she calmly asks. "Why hasn't she thanked you?"

I've sat around many times before, pondering the answer to that very question. To be honest, I didn't have a good reason, except for one. "She was ashamed."

I can tell that she wants me to explain more, simply by looking at the intrigued expression on her face.

"It must have been hard to know that you weren't a parent to your son. It must be hard to realize that a 16-year-old was stronger than you were. A 16-year-old didn't crack under the realities of life, but you did. I imagine that must be hard to remember each and every day."

"And if she says thank you..."

"If she says thank you, then she has to relive all the pain and embarrassment she's felt deep down for all these years."

McKnight simply smiles. "It sounds like you and your mother have something in common."

I smile, and then remember how this conversation started. "You mentioned that my father was my first blaring weakness. Are there more?"

"The smoking has to stop," she bluntly tells me. "Every cigarette simply makes you weaker. I know you believe it's making the pain and anger go away, but in reality, it's pushing it further down, letting it sit there, and waiting for someone to open it."

"You sound like Alex," I subconsciously mutter out.

I instantly freeze, trying not to make eye contact with her, afraid that she'll overreact at the sound of Alex's name.

Her next words are quiet, soft.

"That's all the time we have for today, Mason. I really look forward to seeing you next week."

Chapter 11

The dust fell to the floor as the sound of the power sander drowned out the howling wind outside. Looking through his goggles, Derrick turned off the tool and blew on the wood to clear off the remaining bits. The owl stood, tall and mighty, its wings spread out wide as it soared through the air. He held it up in the light, admiring his best work yet. He ran his fingers through each tiny, intricate detail feeling a sense of pride as he placed it down on the table, next to the others. Every month for the past ten years, these owls have collected in his workshop, each one carefully crafted, painted, and placed around the room. The sense of pride that ran through Derrick's veins served as a necessary escape from the guilt and embarrassment he felt leaving each AA meeting.

As he admired the owl one last time, he heard a knock on the door and it began to open.

"I figured you'd be back here," his wife said to him. "Wasn't a good meeting?"

He sighed, "Ehh…you know how I feel about those meetings."

"Yet you still go," she reminded him gently.

"I know I need to, but I can't stand the idea of these people seeing my mistakes. That's not how I like to live," he told her. "I'm strong, successful, well-liked, yet among those people, I'm a screw-up."

"Being a screw-up doesn't make you any less successful or strong," she stated.

"I need to get through to him," he finally admitted to her. "I can't keep fighting with him."

She laughed, "Maybe you could start by letting him study with whomever he wants."

He started to laugh back, breathing in some of the dust, which turned his laugh into a cough. "Can you believe that? I'm mortified those words even came out of my mouth."

"I just keep thinking," she continued, now hysterically laughing, "about the Derrick I met all those years ago. I wonder what he would have thought of that comment. You know? The one who led equal rights rallies, who studied at Howard." She walked over to him and hugged him.

"I don't think I'd recognize myself," Derrick admitted, his hands covering his face in humiliation. His wife gently kissed him on the forehead. "Oh god, in college, I would have been so ashamed of myself." He picked the owl back up off the table and examined it closely as his wife kissed his forehead one last time and walked toward the door.

"Do you ever think…" he called out to her, "that he doesn't want the spotlight?"

She turned to look at him.

"I just can't help but feel," he continued, "that I'm forcing him to stand in this light that he doesn't want to stand in."

"That boy loves to swim," she reminded him. "You didn't force him into that. If anyone did, it was me."

"Yeah…but the competing…that was me," Derrick admitted. "I don't want this to define him."

"Then don't let it," she told him.

"I love you," he replied to her. "I don't know what I'd do without you."

"Oh, trust me," she answered as she opened the door, "I know. And I love you, too." She went to walk out before he called her one last time.

"Kimmy," she turned to look at him, "he knows I'll always love him no matter what, right?"

She paused for a second, taking a deep breath. It was the first time the two had acknowledged the intuition they held deep down. Choosing her next words wisely, she responded, "I don't know…have you told him?" She smiled one last time and closed the door behind her, snowflakes blowing into the carriage house as the storm outside continued.

Derrick knew deep down, the answer was no. For the past few years, he'd been so focused on Kemarion, his swimming career, and college prospects that he'd completely neglected Dontrell along the way. Derrick couldn't even count on his fingers and toes the number of times he and Kemarion did things together. Baseball games, college visits, movies, they constantly spent time together. With Dontrell though, he couldn't even remember the last moment they spent any time alone. Of course, he didn't know how much he cared about him. He never once took the time to make sure he knew, so he quickly did what his gut told him he needed to do. Grabbing his phone off the table, he dialed his son's number.

Officer McQueen pulled up to the address mentioned on the scanner and carefully looked around the property. Shining his searchlight onto the driveway, he could see the quickly disappearing sets of footprints leading toward the back of the house. Judging by the amount he could count; he'd guess three or four people created them. Leading away from the home, however, were two sets of footprints, much more fresh, barely touched by the falling snow. Following the footprints to the car, engine running and windows fogged, Officer McQueen stepped out of his car and grabbed his flashlight.

The faint light reflecting on the outside of the clouded-up windshield first appeared like the headlight of a passing car. Unlike a passing car, however, this light never vanished, but instead grew larger and larger, flooding the darkness of the back seat with light. Following the light, a tapping on the driver's side window shook Dontrell back to reality. Quickly moving away from Henry, Dontrell panicked as the tapping continued.

"Uhh, one second," he called out, his shaking fingers struggling to throw his jacket on before stepping out into the cold.

"Police, please exit the vehicle, hands where I can see them."

Dontrell looked at Henry—his heart pounding inside his chest—and slowly reached for the handle of the car. He had been trained for this scenario his whole life.

Do not resist.

Do not run.

Do everything they ask.

Dontrell slowly opened the car door and placed his hands up in the air as he exited into the winter night. The snowfall total had increased significantly, piling up easily half a foot from the time the boys left the gazebo for the warmth of the sedan. The wind, however, was more surprising than the snow. Howls of wind blew every few seconds, making the falling precipitation now painful against his face.

"I've got my hands up," Dontrell cautioned to the officer, the level of concentration evident in his face. Officer McQueen stood there, one hand directly out in front of him, a signal to Dontrell to slow down, and the second hand gently resting on his holster.

"Up against the car, no sudden movements," McQueen explained as he used his arm to hold Dontrell against the car. Removing his hand from the holster, he used it to pat down the outside of his jacket and then the pockets of his pants. "Tell me what's in your pockets," he said, his hand resting over Dontrell's phone in his front left pocket.

"It's just my phone...my phone's in the left and my wallet is in the right," Dontrell explained, the wind gusting against one side of his face, while the other was pinned down against the cold roof of the car. McQueen slowly took both out of his pocket and began inspecting his wallet.

"Dontrell Williams…is that you?" he asked.

"Yes sir," Dontrell replied. "That's me, sir."

"Dontrell, have you been drinking this evening…smoking?"

"No sir," Dontrell replied professionally. "I don't drink or smoke, sir."

"You mean to tell me if I go to look around this car, I won't find any drugs or alcohol?" McQueen asked suspiciously.

"No sir, you won't."

"Something tells me I might. Let me ask you this, we received a call tonight about a break-in; you know anything about that?"

"No sir, I don't," he replied. "I was just here at this house earlier. My friend lives here and a few of us were hanging out. I was getting ready to leave, so my friend and I were in the car."

McQueen let go of Dontrell, after multiple inspections of his pockets and the inside his jacket and asked Henry to exit the car with his hands in the air. As Henry exited the vehicle, however, suddenly the look on McQueen's face changed. The fear washed away, and his once tense body posture calmed.

"Henry," McQueen questioned, "are you all right?"

"Yes, Mr. McQueen. I'm all right," Henry responded, his displeasure evident in his tone. "Dontrell was just giving me a ride home…since the storm's gotten so bad."

"This is your friend from school?" McQueen asked.

"Yes…yes, he is," Henry reassured him.

"Be honest with me Henry, have you two been drinking or smoking?" McQueen asked, much nicer than he had earlier.

"No, Mr. McQueen," Henry replied. "We have not been drinking or smoking. In fact, neither of us smoke or drink. If you need to check the car, you can, but I promise you, you won't find anything."

"No, no," McQueen replied. "I don't think that'll be necessary. I trust your word, Henry. Were you both here at this house?" The entire time McQueen is only speaking to Henry, whose eyes kept bouncing back and forth from the officer to Dontrell, still pinned against his own car.

"Yes," Henry told him.

"I received a call earlier tonight about a group of young men who were sneaking around back, the lady was pretty scared and thought it might be a break-in," McQueen told Henry.

"This is our friend's house," Henry explained to him. "She invited us over and asked us to come straight to the basement around back. That's where people will be if you need to confirm it."

"I'll go back and check," McQueen told Henry. "But right now, I'd suggest you two go home. The storm's getting worse and I know your Dad would want you safe." As he said this, he looked back to Dontrell and released his body off the car. He grabbed Henry's hand to shake. "Please say hi to your father for me."

As he grabbed his flashlight and headed up toward the house, Dontrell's shaking hand reached for the driver's side door. Struggling to open it, Henry stepped forward, placing one hand on his back to console him. He felt Dontrell recoil, so he let go and opened the car door with the other hand. The second he opened the door, without even hesitating, Dontrell jumped into the driver's seat. Henry quickly ran around the car and buckled himself into the passenger seat. Dontrell's shaking hands grabbed the steering wheel and started the car, his heart beating so loud he couldn't hear himself think.

"Holy shit," he whispered to himself, as he felt the first teardrop travel down his cheek. He started to drive, his foot stepping down on the gas, heavier and heavier by the second, as the adrenaline flushed throughout his body.

"Deep breaths," Henry told him. "It's over with now. Take a breath and slow down."

"A deep breath?" Dontrell asked, sobbing now. "Did you hear him? He questioned everything I said, but you tell him the same thing and suddenly we're good to go."

"You know he was just seeing if our stories were the same," Henry reassured him.

"He asked you if you were OK?" Dontrell continued. "Like I was holding you there against your will or making you do things you didn't want to do."

"It was only because he knew me," Henry tried to explain.

"No! It's 'cause you are white!" Dontrell blurted out before thinking, letting his subconscious thoughts take control. He didn't expect Henry to understand, but he couldn't be denied his own reality.

"You're scared," Henry said to him, "and that's completely normal, but we need to be happy we're away from the situation."

"We?" Dontrell yelled. "Those suspicious men the officer mentioned? That was JJ, his brothers, and *me*. His brothers were being loud and the old woman next door got spooked by a group of black men hanging out around her house. You have no idea what could have happened if they were in the car with me instead of you. Please don't act like *we* were just in a dangerous situation. You wouldn't have gotten shot."

"No one was going to get shot," Henry tried to soothe him. "Mr. McQueen is a friend of my fathers, he isn't dangerous."

"Do you read the news?" Dontrell asked him. "He isn't dangerous to you, or people who look like you. People like him are *always* dangerous to me and people who look like me."

The car was now hurtling down the small, tree-lined street, with remnants of Christmas lights still illuminating some of the trees. The snow crashed against the windshield, making it impossible to see more than two feet ahead even with the windshield wipers moving left and right at top speed. Dontrell's tears collected in his eyes, blurring the road ahead of him, and his deep-seated anger made his foot a brick against the gas pedal. Suddenly, he heard the light vibration of his phone resting in the cup holder next to him. Looking down, he saw the word "Dad" flash across the screen. A sense of relief flooded over him, knowing his father would understand his reality, but it was coupled with the fear of adding more stress to his father's life. Staring down at his phone, he tried to decide if he should answer.

"Dontrell," Henry stated next to him, but Dontrell's mind was still deciding whether to pick up the phone.

"Dontrell," he said louder now, but Dontrell's anger made him hesitate to answer.

"STOP," Henry yelled out. Instantly, Dontrell looked up at the clear road ahead of him, white snow showering the streets. Then, popping up behind a tree, he saw the red sign. He threw his brick foot onto the break as the car screeched and skidded into the middle of the intersection within seconds. Suddenly, it was like the officer's lights were back, shining into the driver's side window. This time, however, there were two lights, and unlike the officer's, they continued to get larger and larger and were coupled with a loud, blaring horn.

By the time Dontrell looked up to see where the lights and noise were coming from, it was already too late.

———————

Hearing his son's voicemail, Derrick spoke:

"Hey bud, it's Dad, but I'm sure you know that. Listen, I wanted to apologize for today…I shouldn't have been so hard on you. I just see how much talent you have…how much potential you hold. Anyway, I just wanted you to know that it makes me proud, really proud. I know I haven't been the greatest father, but I want you to know how much I love you. I know you've been going through a lot lately and I don't want you to be afraid. No matter what…I will always love you. See you when you get home tonight. I love you, bud."

He hung up the phone with a smile on his face, feeling in his gut that he had just made the first step in fixing the broken relationship with his son.

Chapter 12
March 15th, 2015

The car is parked, waiting outside in the cold March air. The rain begins to fall lightly, a sign of the impending storm to come, but now, it is a gentle warning of the events about to unfold. Standing in the living room, pacing back and forth, I can't help but wonder what the hell is going on.

"You're positive he isn't a serial killer, right?" Dylan asks me, munching on a bag of chips while watching the latest revival of the Real World.

"Yes. I'm positive he isn't a serial killer," I reassure her, but today I'm saying it with much less confidence than I would have yesterday.

"Maybe it's a secret fetish he has, you know? Like he loves women in black dresses or something like that," she says with a mouthful of chips.

"Have I ever told you that sometimes your comments aren't helpful?" I tell her as I grab my jacket and walk toward the door. Touching the handle, I pause and turn back to Dylan. "If I'm not back by midnight, come looking for me."

She gives me a thumb up and a smile as I walk out the front door and throw my jacket over my dress, protecting it from the rain. The dress, the one that I purchased hours earlier, needed to be black. The phone call, cryptic and secretive, gave me two clear directions; no questions asked, and wear black.

I agreed to his rules, purchased a black dress, and asked no questions. It was the first conversation I've ever had with Mason where I could feel a wall between us, and I just can't shake the feeling that today isn't going to be one I'll want to remember.

My wet footprints trace my path from the door to the gate as I head toward the car. Opening the car door, the warmth from inside the car welcomes me much more than the man sitting behind the wheel. Without a smile, without eye contact, Mason turns to me, leans in, and kisses me on the cheek. He's dressed in a suit, a black one, with a dark-toned shirt and tie. It isn't his outfit that makes me question where we are heading, but it's his face. Staring out the windshield, two hands on the wheel, Mason has yet to smile or look me in the eyes.

"Thank you for doing this," he says to me, pulling off the curb and down the street.

"Of course," I reply, watching him.

I look down and can see the pack of cigarettes sticking out of the center console, a lighter on the driver's side floor. He's driving the car, but I can tell his mind isn't on the road. I decide to save the conversation about the cigarettes for another time, as the rain continues to fall, harder now, and we wind through the Brooklyn streets, onto the highway, and head away from the city. A relatively conservative driver, Mason now drives with a sense of purpose, a place to be. The longer we drive, the more questions zoom through my head.

'Where are we going?

Why are you acting weird?

Why won't you tell me what's going on?

Why did I just buy a black dress?'

I remain silent as he speeds down the roads, the increasing rainfall forming a thicker layer of water on the road ahead. The questions pile up in my head, and usually, I trust that they will be answered, but as he continues to drive, I begin to trust him less and less. It's easy to trust someone when they act the way you're accustomed to them acting. It becomes much harder, however, when the person before you, isn't the person they've been.

This isn't my Mason.

My Mason isn't quiet, he isn't curt, he isn't secretive, and he most certainly isn't this reckless of a driver. However, my trust cannot waiver, not now, so I sit, staring out the window, watching the rain continue to fall as we pass exit after exit.

Half an hour later, he exits the highway and takes a few turns down quiet back roads and side streets before finally pulling the car to a stop in the middle of a parking lot.

As he turns the car off, he looks around the almost full parking lot. "Well, let's go," he says to me, still without looking me in the eyes. He goes to grab the door handle and I reach for his arm to stop him.

"Mase, wait," I beg. "Are you going to tell me what's going on?"

He pauses, and I see a glimmer of the man he was yesterday. It quickly disappears and he opens the car door, exiting into the downpour. In disbelief, I follow after him, shuffling two steps behind the entire way, using my jacket as an umbrella. He continues to hasten, unbothered by the rain, puddles, or gusting wind, toward the building.

There are certain smells that belong to specific places and walking into the building, I quickly realize where I am. The smell hits me first. It quickly reminds me of my grandmother's house that always carried this particular scent. The second smell is that of flowers, and not the pretty smell of a bouquet of flowers, but the overwhelming smell of too many flowers confined to a small space.

I have no idea why I'm here, but Mason stands, feet ahead of me, outside a set of propped open, double wooden doors. His suit, water-stained from the lack of umbrella, looks like it is two different colors, and he's motionless, staring directly in front of him. Joining him at his side, I follow his eyes down the long aisle to the large wooden casket resting at the end. Flowers line the aisle, the space around the casket, and the entryway as people fill the seats, crowd in the back, and line up toward the front. The sign next to the door has a picture of a smiling man, his gray hair slicked back, and his mustache perfectly groomed. He's a spitting image of Mason—only much older. The sign reads:

Robert William Bracher
1955–2015

Mason's father.

"This can't be the right place," Mason says, finally turning to look me in the eyes. The veins in his eyes are a blaring red. "I didn't think anyone would be here."

He turns his eyes back to the casket, as I grab his hand.

"I'm here. You can do this," I reassure him, leading him into the room.

The noise is palpable. It sounds more like a college frat party than a funeral. Laughter, smiles, and joy can be felt from the looks on people's faces.

"This doesn't make sense," Mason comments, squeezing my hand even tighter.

A woman, in her late 50s, approaches us. She's wearing a bright, flowered dress, one that seems more appropriate for a spring birthday than a winter funeral. Her smile is loud, stretching from ear to ear. "Hello!" she exclaims. "My name's Patti," as she reaches out her hand to shake Mason's and mine. "How did you two know my Robby?"

I see the blood drain from Mason's face, and my hand can feel his pulse quicken beneath his wrist. Patti stares at us, uncomfortable in our silence and gloomy faces.

"I'm sorry," I interject, "I'm Alex, this is Mason. Mason actually worked with Rob at one point."

I lie. It's the best one I can come up with on the spot.

"Oh, you're an insurance broker? How wonderful! A lot of Robby's coworkers are here," she tells us, as she points to a group in the corner of the room where most of the laughter is coming from.

"Who are all these people?" Mason asks.

"Well," Patti begins to explain, looking around the room, "some are friends from work, some are from our church. The group over there are family friends, and then our kids' friends are over there by the food, of course—typical teenagers."

"Kids?" Mason questions.

"Robby never mentioned his daughters to you?" Patti asks. "I'm surprised. Most people joke that he's probably up there telling all the people in Heaven about them."

Patti begins to look around the room.

"Oh!" she exclaims. "The blonde girl over there, standing by the window, that's our Cassie. She'll be 15 in March…" Patti continues to speak, explaining to us about her second daughter, but the information doesn't matter. You don't need to be good at math to quickly realize that those numbers don't add up.

"She's 15?" Mason questions, clearly having done the math himself.

"Yes! In March. It's crazy how time flies," Patti tells us.

"I'm sorry," I step in, "how long did you say you and Robert were together?"

"We've been married 14 years," Patti says with a smile, clutching the silver necklace around her neck where his wedding band rests. "But together for much longer. I waited quite some time for this ring."

Again, the math isn't difficult and it doesn't take Mason long to figure it out.

"14 years?" he asks, this time forcefully. "Are you kidding me?"

Patti laughs uncomfortably, but Mason presses on, "You've been married to this man for 14 years?"

"I'm sorry," Patti's smile is wiped from her face and she begins to look more serious. "How did you say you knew Robert again?"

Mason laughs loudly, loud enough that the people around us stop their conversations and turn to stare as us.

"How did I know him?" Mason asks aggressively. "Are you seriously asking me that question? I've known this piece of shit my whole god damn life." As Mason speaks, he gets louder and louder. I squeeze his hand in an attempt to calm him down, but there's nothing I can do to stop him. "You know nothing about me, do you?" he screams at Patti. "I bet none of you know anything about me. I bet you don't know my brother Andrew, or my sister

119

Megan, either. I'm willing to bet you know absolutely nothing about my mother, Hannah. God knows he wouldn't tell you about her. Huh? Did he?"

Patti stands there in silence, stepping back as Mason continues to yell. No one is speaking any longer and instead, are all staring in silence at the scene unfolding. "I bet that piece of shit said nothing about us. I bet he never said anything about the pain he caused us, the heartache. That saint of a man you seem to think he was? Yeah, I've got news for you...he was a fucking monster."

Patti begins to cry, still clutching the necklace tightly.

"I'm glad that fucker is dead," Mason finally screams out loud, as he storms away. The room is silent, now that the screaming is done, but everyone still stares, now at me standing there all alone. Patti is hysterical as two older women rush to her side to comfort her.

"I am so sorry," I mutter to her as I turn to walk away, but it is barely audible over her sobs.

Running out of the funeral home, I follow him to the car. Pacing back and forth, Mason looks frustrated, angry. It's the first time I've ever truly seen him mad. I approach but give him his space to move. Back and forth he walks, the rain absorbing into his suit. I simply stand there, watching, waiting for him to show me what he needs because the truth is, I simply don't know. Then I see it, the cigarette in his left hand and the lighter in his right.

The funeral, the family, his father, it's all been quite a surprising day, but none of that even compares to this. The man pacing in front of me is not the man I've known, not the man I've agreed to marry. This man is frantic, unwound, tortured.

He screams, loudly, out into the rainy evening. Then, he cries. The pacing stops, his hands move to his face, and I hear sobs as he falls to the ground. Rushing to his side, I quickly sit down next to him and wrap my arms around him, holding him tight.

"I just don't understand," he cries into my shoulder now.

"I know...I know," I reassure him, rubbing his back.

"They loved him," he weeps, "they still love him."

"Yes. They do," I tell him, his head resting on my shoulder.

"He was a monster," he confesses. "He would come home, throw shit at us, scream in our faces. The piece of shit caused us so much pain. And they fucking love him."

I continue to console him, unsure what to say, but all the while watching that cigarette clutched between his closed fist.

"Fifteen years old," Mason reminds me. "His daughter was 15 years old. You know what that means?"

Unfortunately, I do, but I think it was a rhetorical question.

"For the past 14 years, I have dealt with the pain of him leaving. Constantly questioning whether I was worth it, or what I did wrong. He had a whole second life, a second family. He'd come home, treat us like we were worthless because he always had something better to run to. Who the fuck does that?"

A monster. That's who. Only a monster would treat three children the way this man did. Only a monster would live a lie like that.

"He had a whole different life," Mason repeats to me. "He had friends, he went to church, and he was loving. He did all of that for them. Was I not worth it?"

The question eats at my soul. By this point, the sun has set, but the rain continues to fall. The streetlights begin to turn on one by one.

"I'm so sorry," he whispers to me.

I grab him by the chin and pick up his head so his eyes are meeting mine.

"No," I tell him. He looks down, but I pull his chin back up. "You never apologize for what that man has done. Ever again." Looking into his eyes, I see the pain that envelops his heart. The tears he has cried and the rain falling from the sky have combined on his face, making it hard to tell one from the other.

"I love you," I tell him, "and that means I will stand in the middle of a storm with you. I will never stop standing in the middle of storms with you. We will get through everything…together."

I kiss him and let him rest his head back on my shoulder as he continues to cry. Sitting in a giant puddle of mud, drenched from the rain, in the cold March air, I feel my heart break. It isn't broken by the man I love, but it is broken for the man I love.

After some time passes, I decide to say what I know he doesn't want to hear. "Mase," he looks up at me, "you need to go back inside."

He looks back down at the floor. I didn't know what to expect when I said it, but suddenly I see the man I agreed to marry. He nods his head, takes a deep breath, hands me the cigarette, and stands up. Together, we walk, sopping wet, into the funeral home. The noise has picked back up again inside the room, but Patti is sitting outside, in the hallway, on a wooden bench. We walk up to her, as she dabs her face with a tissue. I urge Mason forward and she looks up.

"Haven't you done enough?" she sobs, wiping more tears away.

Mason sits down next to her. "Patti, I can't put into words how sorry I am. This is such a hard day for you, and I only made it more difficult."

Patti takes a deep breath and looks up at Mason. "It's so hard seeing you here," she confesses. "You look just like him."

Mason pauses, confused. "Wait, you knew who I was?"

"Of course, I know who you are," she tells him. "At one point, some years ago, I put the pieces together."

"But you still loved him?" Mason asks.

"With all my heart," she tells him.

"How could you still love him?"

"We all have secrets," she tells us, "some are worse than others. At the end of the day, I needed to decide if the man standing in front of me had changed. The Robert I knew was not the same man that you knew. It pains me to admit that to you, but he was sweet and loving."

"So you just forgave him?"

"Would you forgive her?" she asks Mason, as she points at me.

Mason looks at me and smiles.

"I would," he tells her.

"Robert was my one true love," she tells us. "When I met him, it was like everything in my life had led me to him."

"What happened when you found out?" Mason asks.

"It wasn't the best moment for either of us. I said some things I regret, things out of anger, but then one day I woke up and my anger was only tearing our family apart more. The guilt your father felt was so great, and my anger wasn't going to change the past. I decided it wasn't worth it."

"But what about us?" Mason asks. "How could you let him live his life without taking care of his own children?"

"I know this is hard to understand," she explains, "but he believed you were better off without him, and it wasn't my place to make decisions for him."

"These all sound like excuses," Mason sighs.

"You're right," Patty says to us. "They were all excuses, but believe it or not, your father was tortured each and every day by the decisions he made in the past. One day, I hope you find it in your heart to forgive him—not for his sake, but for yours. Walking around with that much pain, that much anger, can eat at a person's soul."

Patti gets up and helps Mason up with her.

"Now, I must get back to our guests."

She shakes Mason's hand but then pulls him in for a hug. I smile at her as she turns to walk away. Mason and I stand in the doorway, staring down at the casket resting peacefully at the end of the aisle.

"Do you want to go say goodbye?" I ask him.

Mason pauses.

"Not today," he tells me, "but one day I will." He grabs my hand and pulls me in close, squeezing me with all the love he holds inside. "I love you," he says, "and thank you."

Together, we walk out of the funeral home knowing that the past can never be forgotten, but today it feels a little more forgiven.

Chapter 13
June 25th, 2016

Staring down the long, narrow aisle, unlit candles lining the edges where the white linin cloth will line the floor, I can't help but laugh. The wooden arbor, covered with vines and bright, peony flowers, stands centered at the end of the aisle. The wooden cross-back chairs, lights streaming across the room from one end to the next, the whole scene feels like a dream. Sitting there in the middle of it all, watching the florists finish beautifying the quiet room around me, I can't help but feel like a walking contradiction, a hypocrite. I always prided myself on being this staunch feminist, believing in the idea that women are more than princesses that need saving, but exceptionally strong, independent women who can and will run the world. Yet, here I am dreaming about the perfect wedding with my perfect prince charming. Not to mention that sitting here in this white dress, my hair all pinned up behind my head, I feel like a god damn princess.

Unexpectedly, I feel a hand on my shoulder, and I turn as my mother's smile brightens the room even more. Her dress, long and elegant, makes her look more stunning than I've ever remembered her looking. "It's beautiful, isn't it?" she says to me, as I slide over and she sits down in the chair next to me, her movements not as agile as they once were.

I take in a deep breath, looking around, and reply, "It just doesn't seem like me, does it?"

My mother takes my hand, patting the top as she holds it in hers. "That depends, is this what you wanted?"

I take another deep breath and laugh, "Yes, but that's what I don't understand. I *do* want this."

My mother laughs back, "Well nothing sounds wrong with that." She doesn't stop looking at me when she's finished. Instead, she sits there, doing what she's done best my entire life—reading my emotions. She knows I'm not done thinking, so she waits patiently for my response.

"Do you think he's changed me?" I say, no longer filtering the thoughts running around my head, and knowing deep down that my mother was always free of judgment and filled with honesty. "Do you think he's made me a different person?"

"Yes," she responds bluntly, "I do."

"What?" I respond in disbelief. "How could I let this happen? How did I let a man change who I am?"

My mother laughs at me, "Well, clearly not everything has changed. I have to admit, I don't miss this habit."

"And what's that supposed to mean?" I reply back, offended by her comment.

"You've always doubted your decisions when you're nervous," she tells me, "ever since you were a little girl. You've been the most intuitive person I've ever met, yet you always questioned your gut. For some reason, this word *change* has a negative connotation in your mind. Yes, Mason has changed you, but you have also changed him. And the great thing about your life together is that neither one of you is going to stop changing the other person. For the rest of your life, you will continue to adjust, change, and compromise, so that you can figure out who you are as you grow. Just because you are changing each other doesn't mean it's a bad thing. You are still you."

I squeeze my mother's hand tighter, feeling her wrinkles rub against my skin. "I just never pictured all of this; the white dress, the beautiful flowers, the elegant ceremony. Growing up, this was never something I dreamed about. I never dreamed about being a princess, which is why all of this seems so weird."

"When you were 18," she tells me, closing her eyes like she can picture it so clearly, "I found you one night lying on the bench across the street from our apartment. You were just lying there, staring up at the stars. I sat down next to you, put your head in my lap and just stayed there with you. I knew you'd talk when you were ready. When you were ready, do you remember what you asked me?"

I nod. It's one of those memories that I have always carried with me and probably will for the rest of my life. Samuel had just proposed to me, at 18 years old. Deep down, I knew I was destined for more in life, but I also wondered whether or not he was my true love. I had all these doubts about marrying him, our age being the biggest factor. No one our age had even spoken the word marriage. I had never even thought about it, yet when he asked me, something inside me kept telling me that if I said no, I might regret it for the rest of my life.

"How do you know you truly love someone?" I tell her. "I asked you that question after I told him I needed to think about it."

She smiles at me. "What was my answer?"

"You told me if I needed to ask that question, then I knew the answer," I remind her. I didn't understand her answer at the time, but looking back, it was the best advice she could have given me. "I never wanted a wedding like this because I never truly loved someone enough to marry him."

"And what about now?" she asks me.

"This has been the only thing I've thought about since I met him," I confess to her. "When I look at him, I can't help but picture him old and gray, the pictures of our children lining the walls of our house, sitting in our rocking chairs and laughing about our wonderful life."

She squeezes my hand tighter, grabs my face, and turns it to face hers. Staring straight into my eyes, she asks, "You know why you would have never been truly happy with Samuel?"

For the first time, I realize she doesn't need me to respond back. It's a question she already knows the answer to. It's also a question she probably knew the answer to all those years ago, yet she never pushed or tried to convince me. Her mother's intuition told her I needed to make the decision on my own, and she trusted I'd make the right one.

"You wouldn't have been happy because he wanted you to be someone you aren't," she tells me honestly. "He wanted you to be his princess. Cooking, cleaning, raising a family, that was going to be your job. He wanted to come home every day to a finished meal and a kiss from his wife who would tell him she missed him so much."

As she speaks, I can't help but comprehend the truth behind her words. It's scary to think how unhappy I would have been.

"Samuel wanted someone who needed saving," my mother boldly states. "He was never happy with your free spirit, your independence, your constant drive to be better than you already are. All he wanted was someone who needed him. He liked the idea of having this strong-willed wife, but he needed to be the center of that family."

Confused about the point she is trying to make, I go to speak, but feel my mother's finger against my lips the second they open. I close my mouth and continue to listen.

"Do you believe, deep down, that you are only here today because someone is trying to save you?"

It isn't a difficult question, so I don't need long to answer. "No. Absolutely not."

"Just because you don't need saving, doesn't mean you can't feel like a princess," my mom reminds me. "Don't ever be afraid of your own happiness, my love. Fear can hold you back from becoming who you were truly meant to be. You never dreamt of this before because you never had anyone to stand there with you in your dream. You never had a partner, like Mason."

I continue to watch as the long white carpet is rolled down the center aisle, stopping perfectly at the end of the arbor, and the candles lining the cloth are all lit. My mom continues, "Mason is not your prince or your king. Mason is your partner. There has been nothing about your relationship that has made me believe otherwise. He has continued to support you, through everything you have asked, and you have done the same for him. That does not mean that you should not treat him like a prince and he should not treat you like a princess. Calling someone a princess does not make them weak or secondary, it just means he should treat you like the royalty you are. And I would expect you to do the same for him. There is nothing about your love and life with him that will be easy. The next 60 years of your life will have many difficult moments, moments, at the time, you won't think you can get past, but after every single difficult moment, it will be worth having someone who continues to treat you like royalty."

Looking at my mother, I can't help but smile and be grateful for the life she has provided me. Her love for my father is still apparent in each and every interaction they had, and it has set the foundation for my belief in true love.

A tear falls down my cheek, "Thanks, Mom."

"Now," she tells me much more harshly, as she pulls me up from the chair, "you need to get your butt upstairs, so we can get this wedding started on time. I won't have my daughter be late for her own wedding."

Looking around the room one last time, I hug my mother tightly and head out the door.

Falling into the cushioned chair, my legs burning, the smile on my face won't seem to go away. The room no longer resembles the beautiful ceremony from earlier, but now a giant dance floor overtakes the middle of the room. The music blasts around me, as I watch my mother and father dancing to the music in front of me. Looking around, it is more evident than ever that I am surrounded by love. Our families, our friends, are gathered on the dance floor, living their best lives, and there, smack in the middle, leading the charge is my *husband.*

As elegant as the entire ceremony had looked earlier in the day, looking down the aisle, my father on my left and my mother on my right, it was significantly more special once I saw my prince standing at the end of the aisle. The guests stood around me, all staring at me, but my eyes were locked on the only thing I cared about…Mason. Wishing I was already standing by his side, I hastily made my way down the center aisle, pulling my parents along with me.

Dylan stood there, her smile as wide as ever, and I swear I saw a tear fall from her eyes. Across from her, Kevin placed his hand on Mason's shoulder, and I found myself extremely grateful he chose not to wear the speedo from all those years ago. The most amazing sight to see, though, was the joy on Mason's mother's face. She looked genuinely happy for the first time since I met her.

As I watch Kevin start a conga line, Dylan gladly jumping in behind him, I can't help but think about the vows Mason spoke to me. Written in true Mason fashion, he somehow found a way to express his love in a way I never imagined.

"Before I begin, Mr. and Mrs. Rojas and the entire Rojas family, I apologize if my translation is off. Google Translate was the only source I had available at the time," Mason pulled a paper out of his inside pocket and slowly opened it up.

"Mi amor, Alex," he began, his horrendous accent making my cousins in the back corner of the room laugh hysterically. "El día que nos conocimos, supe que eras mi único amor verdadero. Hoy, quiero que hagas dos promesas. La primera es que prometo seguir demostrando que puedo ser un hombre que es digno de tu amor inquebrantable. El segundo, es que prometo amarte más con cada día que pasa."

The entire right side of the room laughed and clapped while Mason's friends and family sat there with clueless smiles on their faces. "For those of you who don't speak an ounce of Spanish, I attempted to say the following: My love, Alex. The day we met; I knew you were my only true love. Today, I want to make two promises to you. The first is that I promise to continue to prove to you that I can be a man who is worthy of your unwavering love. The second is that I promise to love you more with each and every passing day."

Smiling about the memory, I quickly realize the music has stopped, everyone on the dance floor has stopped dancing, and all are staring at me. Mason, who is standing up at the DJ booth with a microphone in his hand, now has his tuxedo jacket off and his sleeves rolled up.

"I know you begged for no surprises," he says to me as he points to me from across the room, "but this is the last one…I promise." He finishes speaking, the DJ turns up the volume and I hear the beginnings of Tiny Dancer. Right on cue, Mason begins his anthem, and just like our first date, he puts on a show for all the guests watching around us. As everyone around me cheers him on, I know that just like that first date, it never mattered how many people are cheering from the sideline. For the rest of our life, all that matters is that our eyes are on each other.

Chapter 14
Session 4

"Tell me about her," she says, apparently tired of the small talk about the changing weather that has taken up almost half of our session. I fall silent and look over at the owl sitting next to me. Its wings are spread wide, ready to take flight as it hovers above the branch, feet still ready to latch on if it fails. I hope looking away will allow me to avoid responding to her comment.

…it doesn't.

"I've let you take your time," she tells me. "Now, I'm giving you your push." She's right. I hate to admit that, but she is. We've battled it out for weeks, but here we are, in a place where we can be as honest as ever with each other. It's the reason I'm here, and the reason I'll have to keep coming back.

"She's the greatest person I'll ever meet," I confirm for her. "I will go for the rest of my life and never know someone who is as kind, caring, passionate, and just plain funny as she is."

McKnight smiles, probably because I can't help but smile myself. It's one of the few times I've ever smiled in front of her, and it's one of the few times I've genuinely smiled in months.

"When we met," I continue, "she had all these beliefs about me. She constantly misjudged who I was, and probably rightfully so. I'd been that person in the past, and it's like she knew that." I pause, thinking about those moments, the ones ingrained in my memory for eternity.

"What made you change?" McKnight asks.

"To be honest, I don't know," I confess. "I'd like to say it was my dad leaving, but I wasn't a great person after that happened. It's hard to explain. It's like I used up all my love on my family, that I couldn't give it to anyone else."

McKnight nods, a sign that she comprehends my struggle.

"I dated a bunch after he left, I guess to fill the void, but I always treated them the way he would treat us. I wasn't a very nice person. After I moved out, I had a pretty serious relationship. I'd say I was in love, but after meeting Alex,

I know that wasn't true. I can say I liked this girl more than anyone I'd even liked before Alex. When you really like someone, it's easy to put in the effort to make the relationship last. I did everything I could to make her feel special, but then she cheated on me with some asshole from work. I was devastated, but for the first time, I'd been heartbroken by someone other than my father. It woke me up, made me really understand how poorly I treated all those women before her. She was really the first one who forced me to see who I was."

"Hmm…" she sighs in agreement. "Let me guess, you didn't really like what you saw."

"I hated it," I admit. "It was the moment when I realized I was being my father instead of being the man my father should have been."

"So when Alexandra showed up and started assuming you were this person, how'd that make you feel?"

I pause for a second, thinking about the night we met. It's hard to forget because it still is the greatest night of my life. "I felt like she was seeing into my soul," I state. "It sounds weird, I know, but it was like she'd always known me, like she'd already seen all of my faults. Even though she knew all of that, she was still standing there, giving me a chance. It felt like fate."

I start to laugh.

"What?" she asks, genuinely confused.

"That word fate," I tell her. "It's a word I don't think I've ever really believed in until I met Alex. I always prided myself on knowing that I had full control over my entire life."

"Well that's not new information," she reminds me with a laugh.

"I just really believed that all the decisions I made, and all the things that happened to me, were because of my choices. The choices that I had control over," I tell her.

"I'm sure many great things happened to you because of your choices, and many difficult things as well. Many aspects of your life are in your control and can be decided by your choices," McKnight responds.

"But the truth is," I tell her, "it's scary to believe in this idea that there's a piece of your life that isn't under your control. Then you fall in love. You start to think about all of the moments that brought you to that person, and you start to realize they weren't things you chose. Everything that led me to Alex on that night was completely out of my control. It was like an elaborately drawn out plan, a perfectly timed series of life lessons, and a whole lot of luck."

"Ah. Fate," McKnight simply replies. "It can be pretty scary."

I sit there with my hands in my hair, staring at the ground, still in disbelief. I'm laughing to myself, and not because I find it funny, but because I can't believe I didn't realize it before. For the first time since we've started our sessions, I know that Alex isn't the only person who can see into my soul.

"I don't believe in God," I confess to McKnight. "It has been a constant conversation between Alex and me during our entire relationship, but I can never seem to jump on board."

"Why is that?" she asks.

"The whole concept of religion is that this all-mighty being has all the power. Not to mention everything we know about this all-powerful person was written down in a book by a bunch of men who never even knew him."

McKnight laughs with me as I explain my rationale.

"Plus, we live our lives based on what these books say even though they were written so long ago that nothing is the same," I explain.

"So where's your dilemma?" she asks.

"I can't explain being in the same room, at the same time, as Alex," I tell her. "First, I chose to go to Princeton over other schools. Then I just happened to meet my friends at the dining hall one night. Those friends ended up becoming my roommates and helped me decide whether I should move to California or stay in New York after college. I mean, that's the biggest one I can't get over."

"What do you mean?" she asks me.

"I graduated from Princeton," I tell her, "and coming out of college, I had a lot of options. One, though, one in particular, really interested me. I was offered a position with Facebook, out in Palo Alto."

"Wow," she responds, impressed by this new piece of information. "You turned that down?"

I laugh, "Oh, yeah. Today, it's really hard to tell people that I turned Facebook down, but I never liked the website, to begin with. I always kind of felt that if I wanted to know about someone's life, I would have stayed in touch with them."

"Yeah, yeah," she says in disbelief. "What's the real reason?"

"What do you mean?"

"You're what? 30? 31?"

"30," I inform her, "and 31 in a couple of months."

"First off," she begins, "don't you sit here and act all depressed about turning 30. Just wait until you turn 50 and then come talk to me. Second, don't pretend that you didn't know Facebook was going to be huge. Everyone knew by then, so what's the real reason you didn't work there?"

"My family," I admit. "Princeton was two hours from my house. I could be there in no time if someone needed me. California was much farther away. I worried they'd think I abandoned them."

"So, you decided to stay because you thought your family needed you?" she questions.

"Yeah. I did"

"Why did your family need you?" she says to me.

"I'm sorry," I reply, "but that was a joke, right? You seriously can't remember why my family needed me? Do you not remember our conversation from last week about my father walking out?"

McKnight pauses for a second, then restates my words back to me as they begin to sink in. "So you stayed close to home because your family needed you, and your family needed you because your father left."

"My father left," I say, but now I'm only saying it out loud to help myself draw the connection she clearly already made. "My family needed me because he left, so I stayed nearby...because of him." The words slip off my tongue, but my mind is in utter disbelief. For the first time in my life, I can see the connection.

"Fate," she replies back.

"But, it's scary...isn't it?" I ask.

"Depends who you ask," she tells me. "Socrates believed that fate was an idea placed upon us by society. Religious zealots, as you mentioned, believe it's in the hands of our God."

It's an intelligent response, but I'm also beginning to realize it's a cop-out. McKnight doesn't want to answer the question.

"What do you believe?" I interrupt her.

She hesitates. This time, it's a hesitation that shows uncertainty. "I'll be honest," she admits, "I don't know what I believe about fate."

She sighs, places her pencil to her head, and I can tell she's in deep thought about the answer to this question. As she waits, I cannot help but feel an overwhelming sense of connection to this woman. She's the same woman that I've fought for weeks, yet I suddenly feel she, like Alexandra, truly knows how to help.

"I've gone to enough school to know how damaging the word fate can be to mankind. I think of the story of Oedipus and this idea that fate is never wavering. It's the belief that no matter what we say, what we do, or who we love, fate will always make sure it gets its way."

I can't help but laugh. "You know, you would never accept that answer from me. You'd say I was thinking too much."

McKnight leans over, clutching her stomach while laughing. It's the first genuine, heartfelt laugh I've ever heard from her. Once she catches her breath, she responds, "I believe everything happens for a reason. I believe that what we learn is necessary to get us where we were meant to be, so yes, I guess I do believe in the word fate."

It's difficult to think about, though, this idea that things happen for a reason. It's difficult because I don't exactly know what that means for me now.

Is this what fate has planned for me?

"It can be tough, though," she continues, making sure she looks me in the eye when she says this, "to wonder what exactly fate has in store for us. Especially when anger and sadness consume our souls."

I feel my eyes begin to water up, but I use every ounce of control I have to hold them back.

"I know this isn't about you," I begin to say, "but do you struggle to understand why fate decided this was how things had to go?"

McKnight pauses…she takes a deep breath and for the first time since we've met, she looks uncomfortable in her large chair. "It is an idea I struggle with each and every day," she admits.

"Who was it?" I ask. "Who made you question fate's plans?"

McKnight pauses and turns to look at the pictures on the wall.

"What was his name?" I ask.

"Dontrell," she tells me.

For the first time, I understand why McKnight seems to know my every thought and understand my every emotion.

It's because she's lived it…because she's living it.

"Has it been as difficult as you imagined it would be?" I ask her.

"No…" she says, looking down at her hands as she gently rubs her thumbs together. "…it's been far worse."

The answer shakes me to my core, frightens me as I've never been frightened before, but it does not surprise me. Deep down, I knew it would be her answer and I know one day it will also be mine.

"It's just hard," I confess, trying to change the subject, "to wonder why this is the journey we have to travel. I have a hard time thinking that everything happens for a reason."

"I can imagine," she tells me.

For the first time all session, the silence returns. This time, however, it's my fault. The words feel stuck inside my body, unable to escape without the tears that go with them.

McKnight senses my hesitation, senses my emotion and my desire to avoid it at all costs.

"What's one thing that drove you crazy about her?" she asks me.

I find myself immeasurably grateful to her for changing the subject and a smile makes its way back across my face.

"Oh god," I laugh, "she can't walk without making it sound like the floors were going to collapse under her weight."

McKnight begins to giggle as well. "That's it?" she asks me, surprised. "That's the one thing you couldn't stand?"

"No," I explain to her. "You don't get it, she isn't a large person, yet she just walks like a massive ape. I'm telling you, it's impossible to ignore."

McKnight is smiling with me, but never once stops reading my expression, my tone, my choice of words. "What did you love most about her?" she asks.

I don't waste a second, this is an answer I've known my entire life. "She is my purpose in life," I tell her.

"And what does that mean?" she asks.

"On our first date, I told her I felt it was my purpose in life to spend as much time with her as possible."

"Why did you feel that was your purpose?"

"She just has an unwavering ability to see the best in people," I tell her. "I mean everyone. She just seems to firmly believe that everyone deserves a second chance. Heck, not even a second chance, sometimes even third and fourth chances. Every single person who ever wronged her, she'd welcome them back in with open arms. It's unbelievable."

"That sounds like an inspiring quality. I know it's one I wish I had," McKnight admits.

"She's an inspiring person," I say to her.

The expression on McKnight's face slowly changes. It's an expression that tells me I'm not going to like what she's about to say. "Mason," she begins, "I'm so happy seeing you light up when you talk about Alexandra. I can tell how much love you have for her just by looking at your face when you say her name."

It's such a nice statement, but I cringe waiting for the ball to drop.

"I can't help but notice, however," she continues, "that when you speak about her, you use the present tense."

I look at her confused, unsure what she is trying to say.

"Sometimes, when people are unable to admit or accept pain and loss, they cope by continuing to use present tense verbs when talking about the person. Today, you've only spoken about Alexandra in the present tense like she's still here."

I feel the ball drop to the pit of my stomach. The wave of emotions try to overtake my control, try to break to the surface. I feel myself struggling to breathe like I'm suffocating on my own emotions.

"I know it can be hard to hear," McKnight continues, "but in order to make progress, we're going to need to move past the pain, and get to a place of acceptance."

She looks down at her clock quickly, and then back to me.

"Today, we've made great progress, but we have the hardest part of the journey left," she tells me.

"What part is that?" I ask her.

She hesitates, and I can see the empathy in her eyes.

"That part is accepting that she's gone."

With those last few words, McKnight begins to close out our session, but her words are inaudible behind the piercing ringing in my head. It sounds like alarms are blaring, warning me of things to come.

…and I cannot seem to turn them off.

Chapter 15

Kimberly McKnight's black veil covered her face, blowing in the gentle breeze as she stood in the rain, an umbrella held over her head. The seats around and behind her had filled over the past ten minutes, leaving standing room only for those still arriving. On one side of her, Kemarion sat in his black suit holding his mother's hand tightly, and on the other side, resided an empty chair. Her husband stood off in the distance, his shoulders resting against a large oak tree, and his hand tucked into his suit pocket, fiddling with the top of the flask he placed inside earlier that day.

The priest stood in front of the crowd, declaring some belief that God had a plan for everyone and that everything happened for a reason. He spoke of heaven, and about difficult times being God's way of testing his people. McKnight ignored every sound that exited his mouth because the only thing she could focus on was the wooden box being lowered deeper into the eight-foot hole. All she could imagine was her son's lifeless body lying there in that box, his hands folded gently across his chest, his heart still.

You don't tell a grieving mother that her heartbreak is simply a test from above.

Watching the coffin make its final descent into the ground, Kimberly stood up from her chair and grabbed a handful of dirt, squeezing it tightly between her long, black gloves. Kemarion followed, and one by one, they each dropped the dirt into the grave. Turning around, she looked up into the crowd for the first time, seeing the vast number of Dontrell's family and friends stretched out in front of her. It was the boy in the fourth row, however, that her eyes were fixed upon. Sitting there, wiping the tears away from beneath his glasses, his sling wrapped around his left arm, Henry tried to maintain his composure.

Looking at him, all she could think about was that phone call. Dozing on the couch, with the news muted in the background, the ringing of the phone jolted her awake. Everything started out blurry as she looked over at the clock. It was 37 minutes after midnight, which meant her son was 37 minutes late.

Picking up the phone, she struggled to read the name on the caller ID as her eyes adjusted to the light.

"Hello?" she answered, clearing her throat.

"Mrs. McKnight?" The voice on the other line was thin, shaking. "This is Henry Johnson, Dontrell's friend."

"Henry, hi," she responded, confused. "Is everything OK?"

Then, he uttered the words every parent fears, "Mrs. McKnight, there's been an accident."

The panic began to set in, the negative thoughts seeping into her mind, but she pushed them out. This was a time for action, not fear. "Henry," she stated strongly, "where are you?" She heard sobbing on the other end of the phone, but no response. "Henry!" she stated louder this time, "tell me where you are!"

"Weber Road. We're on the corner of Weber Road and Essington. I'm so…" he repeated, but McKnight hung up the phone before he could finish.

Within minutes, Kimberly and Derrick were turning onto Weber Road, the streets difficult to navigate as the snow continued to fall. The eerie scene played out before them as the red lights reflected off the snow, making it look like pools of blood while their son's car remained smashed in the middle of the intersection.

McKnight rushed to the scene, jumping out of the car before it was parked, and rushing past the tape. A yelling police officer tried to call her back as she headed straight for the car. The windshield, shattered into a million pieces, covered the street in front of her, and the driver's side door was completely removed. Looking up, she saw Henry, sitting on the back of an ambulance, getting his arm wrapped in a sling.

"Henry!" she called out, rushing over to him. The second his eyes met her; he began sobbing.

"I'm so sorry. I don't know."

"Henry…Henry…look at me," she tried to comfort him. "None of this is your fault. Where is Dontrell?"

Henry pointed to the second ambulance, where sitting outside the rear doors was a stretcher. From a distance, it looked like a black sheet, but Kimberly could barely make out a lifeless hand hanging off the side. She watched as her husband walked up to the paramedics, and as they folded the sheet back to show him the face belonged to that lifeless hand. Derrick took one look and turned away, hands covering his mouth, sickened by the sight. The second their eyes met; she knew. The look on Derrick's face said it all, and crumbling to the ground, Kimberly wept, as the chaos around her never stopped. Feeling the cold snow beneath her fingers, the coldness spreading throughout her hand making it numb, she fell to the ground. She prayed the numbness would find its way to her heart, but it never did.

As the paramedics moved the body of Dontrell Williams into the ambulance, Kimberly felt his future erasing before her eyes. She wept about all the swim meets she wouldn't be able to attend, the weddings, births, and joyous moments that families were supposed to enjoy together. All she could think about was how each and every one of those occasions would now be celebrated with a caveat, with a sense of pain and sadness because he wouldn't be there with them. As Derrick moved toward her side and placed his hand on her back, Kimberly closed her eyes, and for the first time in her life, she prayed that they would never open again.

With every ounce of strength in her body, Kimberly walked up to Henry sitting at the end of that fourth row and pulled his chin up, so his eyes would meet hers. Then she reached out, grabbed his hand, and pulled him up into an embrace. Feeling her strong, steady hands against his back, Henry sobbed.

"I'm so sorry," he told her, the same words he'd spoken the first time he saw her on the night of the accident.

She responded with the same words she told him on that night, "None of this is your fault."

Guiding him up to the pile of dirt, Kimberly grabbed another pile. "He considered you family," she told Henry, motioning for him to grab a handful of dirt. "So I do, too."

Together, the two dropped another pile onto the coffin while Derrick pulled the flask from his pocket, and took a long sip before putting it back away. Feeling the burn running down his throat slowly helped push his agony down with it and the numbing feeling gave him the strength to stand there, watching his son get covered in dirt as one by one, the guests picked up a handful and dropped it into the grave. He caught their side-eye, as they made their way back to their cars, but he didn't give a shit about what they thought. They'd all get in their cars, express how sorry they felt for his family, and then drive back home to their perfect lives.

He never asked for anyone's pity. Pity was the last thing he wanted because pity couldn't bring back his son. Their pity just made him want to drink even more, so he took another long pull of his flask.

At last, after hugging Henry goodbye one last time, Kimberly and Kemarion made their way over. All that remained by the grave were the empty chairs of those who paid their respects, and all that remained in Derrick's heart was a hole he knew would never be filled again.

"The service is over. Would you like a chance to go say goodbye?" Kimberly asked her husband, the look of sorrow on her face making him sick to his stomach.

"It's disgusting that you'd let him feel like it's all OK," he blurted out, his words exiting his mouth before his brain had time to process them.

"He's grieving, just like you and I," she told him.

"HA!" he blurted out. "He's 17. He's a child. What does he know about grief?"

Kimberly took a deep breath and turned to Kemarion, "Would you go get the car for me, honey?" she said, handing him the keys. As Kemarion walked away, she turned back to her husband, too disappointed to look him in the eyes. "You don't mean that, you're just upset and struggling to find the right way to express yourself."

"Oh, please just shut the fuck up," he told his wife. "Stop being such a god damn martyr. Quit worrying about me and focus on yourself."

Kimberly closed her eyes, taking a deep breath in and out. The slurring of the words, the cursing, and the terrible insults brought her mind back to the beginning of her marriage, long before her husband had been sober. Experiencing them once, however, didn't make experiencing them again any easier. She took one more deep breath, remembering the level of patience she needed to deal with her husband's addiction, before opening her eyes again. "Derrick, I'm going to walk away now. We'll be leaving in two minutes with or without you."

She turned to walk away, waiting to cry until her husband was far enough away so he couldn't hear her sobs.

Looking up at the carriage house, dead vines streaming up the side, with the divorce papers clenched in her hand, Kimberly McKnight couldn't help but feel a small sense of hope. Small pockets of green could be seen developing along with the brown vines, a sign of the emerging spring. In her head, Kimberly believed it to be a sign of the reemerging of her life. The small home, which for so long was used as a space for storage, or as her husband's workshop, now belonged to her. The tiny room upstairs, restructured for her bedroom, felt like a safe haven, an escape from all the pain flooding the home behind her. In her head, she could picture it; books stacked along the back wall, pictures of Dontrell and Kemarion scattered throughout the place, and her favorite new accessories—a leather couch, chair, and side table. It was this space that truly excited her the most. It was there, where her husband's workshop once stood, that she was going to welcome her first client, the first, she hoped, of many, that she will see in her new practice.

Closing her eyes, she pictured Dontrell's face, smiling back at her, knowing that this was what he would have wanted for his mother. It was with that thought that Kimberly McKnight took the first steps up the stoop, through the red door, into her home, and onto the next big chapter in her life.

Chapter 16
October 31st, 2018

My eyes shutter open.

The morning light barely creeps through the window as a pair of ocean-blue eyes stare down at me. His broad shoulders hover above me, every single muscle on his body countable to the naked eye. A body, many would say, built by the Gods but in reality, a body built by a man with unwavering determination. As beautiful as his body is, his face, however, seems to have taken on the stress of the last nine months. His sunken eyes, an indication of his restless nights worrying, the slowly graying hair, a sign of his stressful days with the world on his shoulders, and the fear hidden behind his eyes, a symbol of a man's suppressed emotions. Seeing that I'm awake, the fear behind his eyes disappears, suppressed deep down, and a boyish smile creeps across his face like he's waiting for the good news. It's the same good news he's been waiting for since Friday. Now, four days later, four days of letting him down, I'm forced to let him down again.

"Nothing," I inform him apologetically.

"And that's OK," his unwavering optimism showing no signs of weakness. It's that optimism that continues to put the weight on his shoulders. "It'll happen when it happens."

Easy for him to say.

I honestly don't know what's worse, the feeling of disappointing him or the human foot slammed up against the nerves in my lower back. Both leave me in pain, one emotional and one physical.

"I'm just so uncomfortable," I begin to tear up which is pretty standard at this point. I'm lucky if I can get through the day without having a hysterical breakdown or two. These mini crying sessions are nothing. Yesterday, I balled my eyes out for 20 minutes, snot dripping down my face, hysterically sobbing because the dog wouldn't pee when I took him outside. At least that was in private; even worse was last week when I cried in a public park because the five-year-old in front of me took the last cookies n' cream ice cream bar. Both times, my valiant husband stepped in, put his own needs aside, and only focused on my own. He fixed each moment the same way he's been fixing them for the last eight years since we met.

"Ohhh, I'm sorry," he replies back as he rubs my hand. "What do you need? How can I make it better?"

Of course, I'm the hysterical one and here he is, once again stepping in. Sometimes, I wish that he'd be the mess a little more. Females these days all fight for empowerment, harping on the message that we are capable of being strong, independent people, but the funny part about those women is they all seem to leave out the memories of childbirth. I don't care how strong or independent I may be, childbirth is rough, and I want to be taken care of.

"Not unless you can get this thing out of me," I respond. It's been my typical response for the past four days. I know he can't do it and I feel bad for even bringing it up because I know he's dying inside knowing he can't fix this.

"Are you up for a walk?" he asks. There he is, again, with his unwavering optimism. He knows a walk won't help, but he'll use it as a chance to make me feel better. He read in a parenting magazine that walks could induce labor. Our doctor denies the claims, but my husband never will.

"Sure," I reply, as he slowly helps me out of bed. "Give me a minute to get myself ready, and I'd love to walk with you."

I married my angel.

I know it's cliché to say but I did. Obviously, I believe I do not need a man to be happy, but when I am with Mason, I am unbelievably happy. It's not that I believed the feelings of love and affection would die down, but I honestly never thought they would get stronger as they have over the past few years. Sure, the fact that he is the goddamn energizer bunny may really bother me now, since I have no desire to move fast. It's his energy, however, that has carried us through the last few years. It's not the pregnancy talking either. I've seen women with their husbands. I have friends whose husbands don't even know where the vacuum cleaner is, or how to turn on the washing machine. I have someone that not only knows where those things are but also uses them.

"What do you want to wear?" he asks, knowing my clothes are in the bottom drawer of the dresser and I'm incapable of bending down to pick them out.

"My tank-top and pants should be right on top. I can wear those." I try to respond gratefully, even though I hate how I've been subjected to stretchy clothing for the past five months.

He tosses me my tank top and yoga pants.

"Take this," he says as he tosses me a Yankees sweatshirt. "They have a big game tonight; you want to make sure you show your support."

"I need to show support, or you want me to show support?" I ask back as I throw the sweatshirt onto the bed. He's already out of the bedroom and doesn't hear the comment, so I continue to get ready.

I walk into the bathroom and instantly hate myself. Mirrors aren't your friend when you're 40 weeks and five days pregnant. People say pregnant women glow, but those women aren't five days late.

It wasn't our plan, this pregnancy. Don't get me wrong. I'm over the moon excited and I know he is too, but it wasn't our plan. It's not that we didn't want to have children, but I think it happened a little bit faster than either one of us expected.

Mason obviously took it in stride, never once doubting our ability to make it work. He never doubts our ability to make anything work. Forget the fact that our once spacious home has quickly been filled with baby necessities, he somehow manages to make it feel more manageable than it truly is.

From the day he found out we were having a baby; he was figuring out a way to make everything work smoothly. I remember it was early in the morning and we were both getting ready for work. After waiting around a few days, I finally decided just to take a pregnancy test.

"Don't get your hopes up. It's negative," I remember telling him, walking out of the bathroom and into the kitchen where he was slurping the milk from his cereal bowl.

"And that's fine. We have plenty of time to make many, many babies," he told me.

"Exactly," I said back, but I knew we both weren't convinced. I was afraid to tell him I secretly was hoping it would be positive, but I had a feeling he was afraid to tell me he was also.

Right before we left for work. I heard him calling me from the bathroom. I ran quickly, assuming he was hurt. When I entered the door, he had the pregnancy test in his hand. No, he wasn't holding it the right way.

"You know that's the end I peed on," I told him.

I expected him to drop the test to the ground, but instead, he just stood there holding it out to me.

"I'm not sure if I'm seeing things, but isn't that a second line?" he asked me.

"Don't play this game," I said. "I can't be late for work."

"Al," he held the test closer to my face, "isn't that a second line?"

I remember looking and seeing one very clear, crisp, blue line. Looking closer, I could see a very faint, second blue line running down opposite the first.

"That can't be," I said, looking up at him. "Am I?"

"Pregnant," he announced to me.

It was the happiest moment of my life, easily topping our wedding and the day we met. Meeting this little child has been the only thing getting me through the end of this miserable pregnancy.

I finish getting myself ready and walk down to the kitchen. Mason's standing there reading the newspaper, ready to go. He's got a cup of coffee in one hand and a leash in the other. He hands me the coffee because somehow, he gets enough energy to function without it, and we head out the front door.

Walking outside, the crisp October air quickly makes me regret my clothing options. I suddenly remember the Yankees sweatshirt I threw onto the bed, stupidly believing that I wouldn't need it.

"Here," he says to me, the sweatshirt resting in his hands. "I knew you'd need it." Throwing on the sweatshirt, I realize once again, my husband has thought of everything.

We walk, the dog always two feet ahead of us, and pass by houses eerily decorated with cobwebs, gravestones, and hanging spiders. The wind blows dead leaves along the ground, as Mason's speed continues to pick up. It's been a game we've had going on for the past nine and a half months. He starts out slow, moving at a pace comfortable for me, and then slowly continues to move faster and faster. Eventually, we're speed walking down the sidewalk because apparently getting your heart rate up can also help induce labor.

"Mase," I call out to him, so he realizes I've fallen far behind. "We're going to need to slow this one down."

He smiles and heads back to my side, as we continue at a pace much more to my liking.

"It's a crazy feeling," he tells me. "This idea that one of these days will be a day I remember for the rest of my life."

"You know what else is a crazy feeling?" I ask him. He looks at me, waiting for my answer. "Pushing this baby out of my special place."

He laughs and moves forward to catch up with the dog. I go to take my next step, and the second my foot hits the ground, a searing pain emerges at the bottom of my ribcage. I place my hand on my stomach, bend over slightly, and the pain subsides.

"You coming?" he calls back, already feet ahead of me. I continue the walk, pausing every few minutes as the pain reemerges and then disappears. Mason, oblivious to my pain, continues to talk the entire way home about the history of Halloween, which to him seems like a really interesting topic.

Every couple of steps, I continue to feel this pain. It's not long-lasting, but comes on sharp and begins to fade. The walking gets increasingly difficult and I can feel my breathing becoming more labored. Not wanting to be the girl who cried labor, I just continue to walk, feet behind my husband. The last thing I need is Mason getting his hopes up for false labor.

Arriving home a few minutes later, Mason sprints up the steps to the door of our home. I take my first step up and instantly fall onto the floor, catching myself on the railing on the way down. Mason sprints back down the steps to help me.

"Alex," he calls out, "are you okay? What's wrong?"

I look up at him, searing pain now evident across my face.

"I think it's time."

There's this mixed look on his face, like one of sheer panic, but also a gigantic smile. Instantly, he goes into action.

"Okay, we need the bag," he says, mostly to himself, as he turns to run back into the house.

"MASON!" I call back to him.

He pops out the front door, looking at me, confused.

"Are you just going to leave me outside?" I ask, rather annoyed.

"Oh, right," he runs down to help me back up and gently assists me up the stairs. "So sorry."

The second I hit the couch, he's back to running around like a crazy man. The checklist is clearly memorized because, within minutes, we have my bag, his bag, and the baby's bag lined up at the door ready to go.

"Don't forget the car seat," I remind him.

"It's been in the car for three weeks already," he calls back.

Of course, it has. I don't know why I expected differently. He brings the bags out to the car and then comes back to get me.

"I'm glad you remembered me," I say to him, but he ignores the comment and continues to help me into the car.

As we drive, he runs through our checklist of people to call. We start with my parents, then call his mom, and finally our neighbor who's going to take care of the dog. We're about five minutes from the hospital when he starts to slow down.

"Are you okay?" he asks me.

"Yeah, just a little pain, probably contractions. It's nothing too bad, at least not yet. Why?"

Without answering, he pulls into the McDonald's parking lot.

"You're joking me, right?" I ask.

"What?" he responds. "You just said we have some time and we haven't eaten anything since last night. We need fuel."

There I sit, 40 weeks pregnant, sitting in a McDonald's, attempting to eat a McGriddle sandwich. Meanwhile, sitting across from me is the man who never eats fast food, downing sandwich after sandwich like there will be no tomorrow.

"How are you able to eat at a time like this?" I ask him, disgusted by the amount of food he has devoured.

"I'm stress eating," he tells me, like I couldn't already tell. "We're about to have a baby."

"Totally not trying to be rude here, Mason, but you literally just have to stand there and not piss me off. It isn't a job that requires a ton of energy."

As I speak, a searing pain shoots across the top of my stomach and I scream out loud. Every single person in McDonald's looks over at us in fear as Mason smiles and waves at them.

"We need to go, now," I tell him sternly.

He helps me get up from the table and heads toward the door. I stand there, waiting for him to open it for me, and quickly realize he's no longer next to me. Turning around, I see him back at the table, shoving one more nugget into his mouth and grabbing the chocolate milkshake.

I hope my glare burns a hole right through him.

"What?" he asks, surprised. "You might want this later. I'm just looking out for you."

We get into the car and Mason takes off like a bat out of hell. He continues to speak about irrelevant topics as he speeds down the streets, easily topping 80 miles per hour with the empty milkshake container sitting in his lap. His words are simply noises to me at this point, the labor pains becoming so intense that I can't even hear my own thoughts. I'm panicked that we'll get pulled over, not because of the ticket, but because of the time it would waste. I refuse to have my first baby in a car. The second one, okay, I can handle that, but not this one. Not the first.

Traffic continues to intensify as the early morning rush begins, and for the first time, I'm grateful we no longer live in the city. Any bad traffic out here is worse in the city.

"Get off at this exit," I interrupt him, but he continues to drive past the exit. "What are you doing?"

"We practiced this," he reminds me. "Twenty-three is the best exit to take. It's the straightest route to the hospital."

"I don't want straight, I want fast!" I yell. "Don't make me take over the driving too!"

Like a good husband, he ignores my outburst and continues to drive. In hopes of calming me down, he slowly turns the radio dial up, but I slam my hand down against the power button turning it off completely.

147

After minutes of silence, he pulls off at exit 23 and makes the straight shot to the hospital. Deep down, I know he was right, this was the best route, but I'll never admit that to him. At least not now.

The emergency entrance is vacant, making it easier for us to pull up and get out of the car. Mason tosses the valet the keys and grabs the bags from the back.

"Wait!" I tell him. "Wait, just wait."

"What?" he asks. "What do you need? What's wrong?"

"My books, I forgot my books. I'm going to need books to occupy me." I inform him.

"I have three books in the bag already," he tells me. "Do you really think with everything you've got going on that you need more than three?"

I hesitate to think about my answer. "There's a new one, though, one that I bought last week. You forgot it at home, so we need to go get it."

Mason opens the bag and pulls out the new book. "It's right here. I've got it already."

"Yeah, but my comfortable sweatpants, they're on the dresser at home."

Again, Mason goes digging through the bag and pulls out the sweatpants.

"My phone charger."

He pulls out three.

"My laptop. What if there's an emergency at work?"

He points to the backpack. "Tell me what's really happening?"

Suddenly, in the middle of the emergency entrance to the hospital, I begin to sob. This isn't a cute couple of teardrops; this is an all-out downpour of sobs. Snot, tears, ugly faces are all happening at the same time.

"Can't you just push it back up?" I beg him. "I can't do this."

He laughs. "I don't think that's possible, Al."

"I'll go have sex with you in the bathroom," I tell him; rubbing his six-pack beneath his shirt. "Maybe that could force the baby back up."

"I'm not an OB/GYN, but I don't think that's how this whole thing works. Look at me," he tells me as he grabs me by the shoulders. "Deep breaths."

He stands there with me, the valet driver staring at us like we're an engaging reality show, taking deep breaths. My sobbing slows down, but a searing pain shoots across the top of my stomach again.

"Yep. OK. Let's go," I tell him, hunched over in pain as I walk through the hospital doors. Of course he's still standing there, in the middle of the entrance ramp, staring out into the world.

"What are you doing," I yell to him. "I'm good! Let's go!"

He comes running back next to me, taking my hand and guiding me inside.

"What the hell was that?" I ask him.

"The next time we leave this hospital, we'll be parents," he tells me. "I wanted to remember the moment."

Normally a sweet gesture, I simply roll my eyes as the pain becomes unbearable and I signal the nurse for a wheelchair.

"Good morning," Mason calls out to the nurses behind the desk. "Alexandra Rojas, checking in to have a baby."

A nurse walks up to the front of the desk, the bags under her eyes and the blank expression on her face a sign of the long shift she is about to finish.

"And you're Dad?" she asks Mason. I see that boyish smile from earlier this morning creep back across his face. He stands up a little taller, prouder.

"Why yes, ma'am. I am Dad," he replies back. I'll admit, even with all the pain, that word sends chills throughout my body. It's the first time I've heard anyone use the word in reference to Mason.

It's exciting.

Unfortunately, the nurse doesn't find it too interesting, as she ushers him over to the side and hands him a stack of paperwork.

"Fill these out, please. I'll walk you both to your room," she says to him. Mason grabs the paperwork and walks back to the wheelchair. I can see a tear forming in the corner of his eye.

"I'm going to be a Dad," he reminds me.

All I can think you myself is: Thank God I found you.

Hours upon hours we sit there, the pain only continuing to get worse, waiting for my body to be ready. The Yankee game, an evening playoff game, is already in the fifth inning. I find it difficult to pay attention, with the medicine making it easier to nap than watch a baseball game. Mason, on the other hand, sits there anxiously, watching every second, not knowing what else to do while he waits. I'm praying that the baby comes before the game is over because I can't possibly imagine waiting here for four more innings, but I know he's hoping for the opposite. Thankfully, shortly after the inning ends, the doctor walks into the room and begins his exam. Mason stops watching the game, grabs my hand, and waits at my side.

"Well," the doctor says, as he removes his gloves. "How would you two like to have a baby?"

"Please tell me we're ready," I beg.

"I'll go page the nurses, and we'll get this show on the road," the doctor says with a smile before he heads into the hallway.

Time passes, and I'm pushing harder than I've ever pushed in my life. The doctor continues to give me praise, like telling me I'm doing a good job will make this any easier. Anxious to stop the pain and to see the child I've been growing for ten months; I scream and scream. I can feel the bones in Mason's hand crumbling under the pressure of my squeeze.

Suddenly, without warning, the room fills with the cries of a baby. Sweat beads down my face, my hair sticks up in multiple directions, but my eyes-only focus on the child being presented to me. Mason's sitting at the side of my bed, holding my hand and we're watching, as the most precious baby I've ever seen gets placed on my chest.

"Congratulations," the doctor says, "it's a girl."

I start to cry, hysterically. I don't cry out of pain, but pure blissful joy. Mason kisses my forehand and then the baby.

"Does she have a name?" the nurse asks.

Looking up at Mason, his smile warming my heart, I share her name for the first time.

"Sophia," I inform the nurse. "Her name is Sophia."

"Such a beautiful name," she tells me, as she begins to clean up the area around us.

She cries—a weak, newborn cry, as I hold her tightly to my chest. My love for Mason, an ever-growing love, was the greatest love I ever believed I'd feel. Looking into the eyes of this beautiful baby, however, I quickly realize that my love for him cannot even compare to my love for her.

Mason takes her from my arms and pulls her close to his chest. I lay there, watching him smile at her. Then I hear it, it's the faintest whisper coming from his mouth.

He's singing.

You are my sunshine, my only sunshine.
You make me happy when skies are gray.
You'll never know dear how much I love you.
Please don't take my sunshine away.

As he holds her, I can begin to picture her future. I see toys spread out across our living room floor and laughter that fills a room and melts all hearts. I can see her falling in love for the first time, experiencing heartbreak, sipping hot chocolate on a cold winter night. All the while she was growing inside of me, I could never picture all of this, but seeing her, looking into her eyes, I feel I can sense her entire life.

In every moment I picture her in, Mason is there by her side.

I, however, am not.

Chapter 17
Session 5

You're standing at the edge of a cliff. It is deep, jagged, and the bottom seems endless. Deep down, you know the truth. You know that what you need to survive is there, down at the bottom of this vast darkness. Without it, the person you were, the person others need you to be, cannot exist. Without it, the evils threatening to ruin your very existence will prevail.

Life, your life, depends on you getting to the bottom.

…but it looks like it has no end.

What do you do?

Do you stay standing, at the edge of the cliff, hoping that you can continue to survive without what you need? Or do you take the leap of faith, knowing whatever meets you at the bottom has to be better than the reality of today?

Standing outside the vine-covered cottage, I find myself pondering these questions. Turning and walking away is like standing on the edge of the cliff, and never taking the leap. Walking up the stoop, and knocking on that red door though, is taking the leap and praying that everything turns out all right. Walking up this stoop, knowing that my darkest day will be relived, is the scariest leap of my life.

But I stop to think of Sophia.

If I turn, walk back to my car, and drive away, I know the man that will raise her won't be me. A shell of myself will exist, will be there for her, will raise her, but she won't get the man she deserves as her father.

Thinking about my daughter, about the man she needs me to be, the man she deserves as a father, I walk, step-by-step up the stoop with the bold, red door standing in front of me, and I knock.

McKnight opens the door with a smile. She doesn't mutter a "hello" or a "nice to see you." She simply smiles, opens the door, and waits for me to enter, but I stand, hesitating on the stoop before forcing my left foot to take the first step forward. Noticing my hesitation, McKnight begins to close the door, forcing me to enter the home faster.

The owls, relocated again, seem to stare at me as I move toward the couch. Without making eye contact, I sit down across from McKnight. The owl to the right of me is now in full flight, wings out as far as they can reach, soaring through the air.

I can't help but think about how nice that must feel. Flying through the air, no natural predators to worry about must feel breathtaking and calm. I close my eyes, imagining what it must feel like to soar above the ocean, the wind blowing beneath my wings, the sun setting on the horizon. To fly into the sunset, not concerned about tomorrow, or yesterday—only worried about what's in front of you. It's ironic that the ability to remember our yesterdays and hope for our tomorrows is viewed as a strength in humans. We learn from the mistakes of our past, remember the lessons, and apply them to our future success. Lately, however, it seems to be more of a weakness.

What if we could just forget our yesterdays, and only focus on today? I wonder if that would make us stronger.

"Tell me about your thoughts," she says to me, breaking the silence that has lingered, and bringing my thoughts back to reality. I shouldn't be surprised at this point in our relationship that she doesn't need me to speak to know what I'm thinking. Simply sitting on that couch in silence and watching me has helped her learn more about me than most people will ever learn.

"I'm thinking about our weaknesses," I tell her with a laugh. I don't feel afraid to speak as I did so many weeks ago. It isn't the fear of appearing weak that frightens me anymore. I've accepted the fact that McKnight is stronger than I will ever be. Today, instead, I'm worried about being able to continue to live.

She smiles, not surprised that my mind went straight to strengths and weaknesses. "Well, what's the definition of a weakness?" she responds, her smile stretching even wider. She knows comments like that drove me crazy weeks ago, but I've grown accustomed to them over the past few weeks.

Thankfully, I don't have to answer. She has an answer of her own. "I know what you're thinking. You want to give me the definition of weakness. You want to tell me that weaknesses are a disadvantage, a fault that causes humans suffering, or defeat. You want to tell me that a baseball player, whose weakness is to hit a slider, is less effective, less valuable, than a player who can. Isn't that true?"

It was exactly what I was thinking. Well, except for the baseball analogy, but I like it. It's just further proof that I don't need to speak for her to know what I'm thinking.

"Absolutely. That's exactly what I was going to say," I reply. "Every pitcher that player faces knows to throw the slider. They pick apart his weakness."

She's working an angle, and I know it. I don't mind at all. I'd much rather talk about baseball. It's like going to a doctor to get a shot. Most doctors will tell you they're going to count to three and then stick you with the needle. They count; one, two, three, and then they stick it into your arm. McKnight isn't most doctors. She's the doctor who tells you she'll count to three. She'll start; one, two, and then she'll stick it into your arm. She knows that when she waits until three, the patient knows it's coming. They clench their fists, their arm is no longer relaxed, and the shot actually hurts more.

Just wait. Right now, she's only at one.

"So every pitcher continues to throw him the slider, over and over and over again, just to exploit his weakness," she continues my explanation.

"Exactly."

"Until?" she asks, and then pauses, making it clear that she will not be answering this question on her own.

"Until he hits it," I inform her, assuming that was the answer she wanted to hear.

"Now," she continues, "that player who couldn't hit the slider has seen so many sliders that his weakness has become his strength. He has had the opportunity to practice over and over again. His failure led to his greatest success."

I should have known the conversation would lead here.

This is her number two.

"What weakness were you thinking of exactly?" she asks. Now that her point has been made, I can tell she's anxious to pick apart my thinking.

"Our inability to live day to day because of our constant fear of our yesterdays and tomorrows," I tell her, running my fingers along the arm of the leather couch.

Breaking eye contact with me, McKnight stares off out the window. She sits back in her chair, crosses her legs, and puts her hand to her face. As she ponders my last words, silence envelops the room once again.

Finally, after some time, she speaks.

"What do you see as some benefits of living day by day, with no knowledge of the past or concern for the future?" she asks.

"Well," I tell her, "an inability to remember the past would mean that a baseball player who can't hit sliders wouldn't remember that he can't hit sliders. Every time he stepped up to bat, he wouldn't be worried that a slider would come his way."

I go back to the baseball reference just to make the explanation clear, and as I continue, McKnight watches me, pencil resting on her lips. "A baseball player who can't fear for the future won't worry about having to hit the slider. He would just focus pitch to pitch. He doesn't know his weakness, so he isn't afraid of failure."

"How does that make him stronger?" she responds confusingly. I begin to get the sense that we are approaching this conversation from two different sides.

"There is no fear, no worry, no concern. All he has to do is focus on what's right in front of him," I tell her, my hand gestures picking up speed as I begin to get frustrated that she isn't comprehending my point.

"He'll never be able to hit the slider," she responds back firmly, using her own hand gestures in response to mine. The conversation is starting to feel like a baseball argument I would have with my brother, not a therapy session.

Just wait for the needle.

"What do you mean, he won't be able to hit it? He has a chance to hit it each time he bats, but without the fear of it," I inform her. I can feel myself, my heartbeat quickening, and my pulse can be seen ticking underneath my skin as my blood pressure begins to rise. The blood flow to my face increases and it becomes redder by the second, but McKnight sits back in her chair, as calm as she's ever been. It's like her heart is a steady metronome, beating consistently no matter what is happening around her.

"Look at your hands," she tells me, with a smile across her face.

I look down at my hands, confused by her statement, but I quickly see what she wants me to see. Rested firmly on my knees are both my hands, fingers spread out, wrists relaxed.

"Now," she continues speaking once I look back up, "if you were unable to remember your yesterdays or think about your tomorrows, your hands would be clenched into fists right now. Your heart, which right now has quickly calmed itself, would still be rapidly beating. Your face, swiftly back to its normal color, would be beet red and I'd be able to hear you breathing from here."

I instantly notice how my heart has calmed itself, and how my breathing has remained consistent and steady. I don't feel that hazy fog clouding my judgment. Instead, my mind is clear.

"Your yesterdays allowed you to adapt, to grow, to adjust to a situation. Your ability to remember helped a weakness become a strength. You, my friend, just hit a slider."

God damn it. There's the needle.

Somehow, no matter what, she finds a way to bring the truth to light. Seeing her opening, she works the conversation to the topic she knows we need to discuss. "Speaking of remembering your yesterdays," she begins, "tell me about that day at the hospital."

Stuck, frozen, I sit there and stare at her. It's a place I've struggled to bring my mind to each and every day. Knowing that this is where we've been heading, I've tried to prepare myself, but when she says those words, I can't help but feel a deep sense of fear.

"I know," she tells me, "I know how hard it is to go there. It was a place I never wanted to go myself at one point in my life, but you and I both know that we need to talk about it."

Closing my eyes and taking a deep breath, I try to begin to tell her my darkest reality. The instinct to withhold the information, to avoid the topic, I can feel it bubbling deep within me.

This is the cliff, and I know I need to jump, but it just seems so hard. Then I see Sophia's face, staring up at me as I feed her a bottle. I see her innocent, green eyes, identical to her mother's, and I know I have to jump, no matter how scared I am.

"We've talked before," I begin to speak, my voice shaking, "about being torn between two emotions, and sitting in that realm of confusion. That day makes me so incredibly happy sometimes, but also, it takes me to places I never want to go."

For the first time since I have walked into this office, I grab a pillow sitting next to me. The softness, the comfort of the pillow, reminds me of her. Squeezing the pillow to my chest, I continue telling her my truth.

"Every time I walk into Sophia's room, and I see her angelic face smiling back at me, I find myself feeling this pure, unwavering, blissful happiness. That wide-eyed, open-mouthed smile makes me feel like the luckiest man in the world. The way her eyes light up when she sees me, the way she stares into my soul, I can't help but feel the love for her encompass my entire body. It makes me want to be someone she's proud to call her father."

Holding back the tears, I feel my chest begin to tighten. "But I can't be," I tell her.

She grabs a box of tissues sitting next to her, leans across, and places them on the couch next to me. I continue to stare down at the floor, afraid that looking into her eyes will only make this story harder to tell.

"I can't be that man because that man doesn't exist anymore. At one point in my life, and even for a few brief minutes of hers, I believe that man existed. I believe I had the ability to be a truly amazing father." Unable to hold them back any longer, I feel the first tear begin to make its way down my face. It's cold, and I can feel that cold as it makes its way down my cheek before falling off my face to the floor below. Before I even get a chance to start to speak again, I can feel the second one begin its descent. There is no stopping them now. "And then my world stopped," I confess. "My heart stopped working."

I look up and see her, looking at me with a level of understanding I haven't seen in a very long time. Alex used to talk to me about the difference between sympathy and empathy. This woman, the way she looks at me, the way I can sense her sorrow beneath her brown eyes; empathizing with my story, she waits patiently for me to say the words I've yet to say out loud. The words I didn't believe I had the strength to say. She nods, lightly, an inspirational nod, a nod that tells me I can do this. She is a survivor, I remind myself, and I can be one too.

"I was sleeping," I continue, this time looking her straight in the eyes, no matter how much it hurts. "Alex had begged me to mute the monitors because they beeped constantly and made it so difficult to sleep. We were so exhausted, and they just beeped all day long. Every time Sophia would fall asleep, they'd start to go off and she'd wake up every few minutes and just cry endlessly. We'd been up since the day before. We needed sleep."

My body begins to shake. "I was so tired. I had to turn them off." The guilt only causes the tears to come faster. Grabbing a tissue, I keep going. "At some point, I woke up to the sound of Sophia crying. From a distance, Alex looked like she was fast asleep. I got up to get the baby, to bring her to Alex to eat. Once I got closer to the bed, I could see paleness in her face, like a gray darkness was spreading throughout her body. I pulled back the sheets to grab her hand, and that's when I saw the blood, stained into the sheets. I knew something had gone wrong. I ran into the hallway, screaming for the doctors, for anyone, to come and help, a wailing baby still in my arms waiting to be fed. The nurses came and quickly kicked me out. The doctor was quickly behind them. I'll never forget how he looked at me, before he walked in, and told me he'd come to update me the second he could. I was just standing there, in that cold hallway, holding Sophia as she cried, confused about how all of this was happening."

I take another deep breath, hoping it will help me continue my truth. "A few minutes later, the doctor came out. Looking at his face…that was the first time the fear crossed my mind. He explained to me that at some point, someone missed the fact that part of Alex's placenta was never removed. It caused her to bleed out and…"

Unable to continue, I place my hand to my face, fingers in my eyes to try and stop the crying. McKnight gives me the time I need, as I pull myself together.

"…and she didn't make it," I finish my story, wiping my eyes with a tissue, and the silence feels welcoming as I work to pull myself together.

A few seconds pass and McKnight begins to speak. "How did that feel? Getting those words out?" she asks me.

"That's the first time, the first time I've told the story," I confess to her. "It's the first time I've cried about it, the first time I've truly felt it."

"Why do you think that is?" she wonders.

"I just felt so angry, so incredibly angry. I couldn't get past the anger to even feel the sadness. There are reminders of her everywhere—like every morning that I wake up, wishing I could roll over and see her, and every night I go to bed, wishing I could kiss her goodnight."

The tears build up again. "I miss my wife," I sob, still wiping them away. "She promised she'd be there for all the storms. She promised me a lifetime. I'm 30 years old, and have a daughter, and…I'm a widower. I'm going to have to spend the majority of my life without her, but I can't do this without her," I confess. "I can't be the guy she helped me become without her. I can't be the father I need to be without her."

"Why is that?" McKnight asks. "Why can you not be the father this girl deserves?"

This…this kills me to confess.

"I look at that girl and I see my wife," I explain to McKnight. "Every time I see her, I'm filled with this immense feeling of love, but it's followed by a feeling of loss. Every time I see her, I'm reminded that I am completely alone. Every time she cries in the middle of the night, I'm reminded that I'm alone. Every time I feed her, I'm reminded that I'm alone. She makes me relive the one day I want to forget."

It's a soul-crushing confession. This idea that I can't even look at a little girl—a beautiful, happy, little girl—without reliving my greatest pain.

"It makes me hate her sometimes," I tell her embarrassingly. "There are times when I hate her because she makes me remember."

I let go of the pillow, placing it back down next to me on the couch, and take deep breaths to pull myself together. I notice my breaths are lighter, like a giant weight has been lifted off my shoulders, and it feels easier to breathe.

"I just want to forget," I plead to her, hoping she will wave her magic wand and make all my pain go away. "I want to forget the love I felt for her, so I don't have to live with this heartache."

"That is a feeling," McKnight begins, "that will never go away. You will continue to wake up each morning and go to bed each night, missing your true love."

I nod, knowing it's the truth. There is no magic wand.

"You also, however, get the blessing to wake up each morning and go to bed each night, with the love of a child. That beautiful baby that you care for each day, that girl deserves every ounce of love you have to give. She deserves the man you know you can be."

"How do I do it?" I ask. "How do I become that man again?"

She pauses, deciding how to best explain the answer to my question. "You need to talk about your wife," she tells me. "For weeks, you've been avoiding having the tough conversation that you need to have. Today, you took a big step forward. You opened up your Pandora's box in a safe, controllable environment."

"It just hurts too much," I remind her.

"That's because you've only focused on the pain," she begins to explain. "Do you remember how you felt, the day we spoke about Alexandra together?"

"I felt happy," I inform her. It's easy to remember because it was the first day I felt true happiness in months.

"Exactly! You've spoken about her before without thinking of the pain. You remembered her for who she was, what she meant to you. That is the Alex you need to talk about."

"So I'm just supposed to ignore the pain?" I ask her.

"Never. You are always going to remember that pain. There is no way that the pain goes away. There is, however, happiness that can outweigh the pain. That is the happiness your daughter needs. Your wife is so much more than that moment. She lived a life that deserves to be talked about. She loved a man and that deserves to be talked about. Most importantly, she loved that little girl, and *that* needs to be talked about."

It's a point that I've never considered up until this very moment in time. All this pain, this darkness, has overtaken my soul. It has created a man that I was not destined to be. This pain, this darkness, it forced me to only see the bad, and nothing else. Darkness only creates more darkness. The more I thought about the pain, the more I held onto the pain, the more I pushed it down into my soul, the more difficult it became to be happy. Speaking my truth, telling my story, sharing my pain, it's the only way I can get it out. The only way I can let the glimmer of light begin to break through.

It's the only way I can be the father I need to be.

"I'm just so afraid of what's next," I willingly confess to her.

She pauses, again, in an attempt to ensure her words are spoken correctly, her message received. After a few seconds, she sits back in her chair and begins to speak. "We spoke on your very first day," she reminds me, "about the reputation of the owls. We argued over this idea that some people think intelligence is convincing people you are smart and others think intelligence is shown through overcoming challenges."

She looks around the room at the owls and then down to the one next to me. "You walked in this room pretending you were smart. You acted like you were OK, and that made you weak. Today, you've shown your true strength. Today, your intelligence was shown through the challenge. You want to be the man that girl deserves?"

"I do," I respond back confidently.

"Then stop pretending," she bluntly tells me. "Stop pretending everything is okay because it isn't. Be real. Feel anger, feel sadness, and feel joy. All of those things are okay to feel. Your strength comes from understanding your weakness. Own it."

She stops, looking back to the owl next to me. My gaze ends up focused on it, too. It's funny how such a small object can be the focus of so much conversation.

"The owls," she says to me.

"What about them?" I ask back.

"There are only five different owls," she confesses to me. "Even though they are all designed and painted differently. There are only five different actions the owls take."

She points to an owl on the fireplace. "The first rests on the tree, closed off to the world around it. The second," she points to one on the bookshelf, "begins to spread its wings, but is still confined to the branch it sits on."

I follow her hand as she points to the third owl on the windowsill. "This third one has decided to spread its wings wide, finally open to the possibility of flying, but still afraid to fully let go of the branch. Then there is this one," she points to the one sitting on the table next to her, "it has finally decided to push itself off the branch. It has decided that flying is worth the risk, but it is afraid to go too far."

Finally, she points to the one next to me. "And the last one, the last one is realizing that all along, it was afraid of doing something great. Flying is what it was meant to do. If it had stayed on the branch, never taken the risk, it would have never realized its true potential and never enjoyed the greatest joys in life."

Finally, her voice gets low, as she leans in closer to me. "You shouldn't be afraid to reach your truest potential, otherwise you may miss out on the greatest joys of your life."

She pauses and looks at me with a smile.

"That's all the time we have for today, Mason. I look forward to seeing you next week."

Standing on the stoop, the red door closed behind me, I look out into the labyrinth in front of me. No longer do I reach into my back pocket for a cigarette. Instead, I breathe deeply, feeling the cool air enter my lungs as they expand. I exhale slowly, feeling my pulse beating steadily against my skin. The world in front of me is scary. It is painful. I realize that I will never live without fear. Fear of my yesterdays and fear for my tomorrows will always exist. It is my choice, however, how much that fear controls me.

Getting to my car, I turn back to look at the cottage, hidden behind the bushes, but just slightly visible to the eye that knows what it's looking for. I notice the browning vines beginning to show patches of green, patches of life beginning again after a long winter, and I can't help but feel like it represents a symbol for my own life. My own winters, filled with darkness and cold, are slowly moving behind me, but with the passing winter come the promises of a new life, a new life slowly beginning to emerge.

I feel the fear that this new life holds, but then the image of Sophia's face crosses my mind.

…and suddenly I am no longer afraid.

CPSIA information can be obtained
at www.ICGtesting.com
Printed in the USA
LVHW021008040121
675397LV00008B/600